ALONE IN PARIS

Barbara Cartland

ALONE IN PARIS

Thorndike Press • **Chivers Press**
Thorndike, Maine USA   Bath, England

This Large Print edition is published by Thorndike Press, USA and by Chivers Press, England.

Published in 1999 in the U.S. by arrangement with International Book Marketing Ltd.

Published in 1999 in the U.K. by arrangement with Cartland Promotions.

U.S. Hardcover 0-7862-2084-8 (Romance Series Edition)
U.K. Hardcover 0-7540-3888-2 (Chivers Large Print)
U.K. Softcover 0-7540-3889-0 (Camden Large Print)

The text of this Large Print edition is unabridged.
Other aspects of the book may vary from the original edition.

Set in 16 pt. Plantin by Al Chase.

Printed in the United States on permanent paper.

British Library Cataloguing in Publication Data available

Library of Congress Cataloging-in-Publication Data
Cartland, Barbara, 1902–
    Alone in Paris / Barbara Cartland.
      p. (large print) cm.
    ISBN 0-7862-2084-8 (lg. print : hc. : alk. paper)
    1. Large type books. I. Title.
    [PR6005.A765A79 1999]
    823'.912—dc21   99-28410

Author's Note

Throughout the world the Moulin Rouge became the synonym for Paris — another word for pleasure.

It was the heart of the great erotic myth of a naughty, free, uninhibited city of *frou-frou* and champagne, of love and laughter, of poets and painters. The golden age of the Moulin Rouge lasted for five years.

La Goulue soon gave herself the air of a Prima Donna. On one famous occasion, she insolently addressed the Prince of Wales, by then a devotee of Paris — by calling out:

"Hey, Wales. It's you who's paying for the champagne."

By the end of the century she was a Circus performer in a lion's cage and a few years later, gross and prematurely aged, she was penniless.

'Degeneration' by Max Nordau was published in 1893 and was a sensational best seller.

1892

I

As the train began to slow down to enter the station the Governess in charge of the three girls in the carriage, turned to Una.

"There will be somebody to meet you?" she asked in her prim, yet rather indecisive voice.

"Yes, I am sure my father will be there," Una replied, "I wrote to him a week ago, saying I would be on this train."

"That is all right then," the Governess said, with a note of relief in her voice.

She had obviously been apprehensive when they left for France at having three young ladies in her care, but Una had been so helpful and so polite that Mademoiselle had warmed to her and in fact, found the journey had been far more pleasant because she was with them.

The other two girls, daughters of the Comte de Beausoir, were high-spirited and obviously bored with the Mademoiselle who had taken care of them in the holidays.

The youngest of the Comte's family,

Marie-Celeste, who was only fourteen, was always mimicking the Governess behind her back and was a continual cause of anxiety.

Una had sensed that Mademoiselle, who was getting on in years, was clinging to her position in the Comte's household simply because it was familiar and she had no wish to start all over again with another family.

She was therefore far more lax with her charges than she should have been and Marie-Celeste had made the long journey one of anxiety from the moment they left Italy.

Now they were arriving in Paris and Una was, in fact, more sorry to say good-bye to the woman with the anxious face than to the two girls who had been fellow pupils with her at the Convent where she had spent the last three years.

It seemed strange, she thought, that having not heard from her father for so long, he should suddenly have sent her a telegram in response to her last letter, saying:

"Come at once! No. 9 Rue de l'Abreuville, Montmartre, Paris."

She had taken the telegram to the Mother Superior who had frowned at the address.

"Your father lives in Montmartre?" she enquired.

"Yes, Reverend Mother," Una replied. "As you know, he is an artist."

The Reverend Mother pressed her lips together as if it was with an effort that she did not say what she thought not only of artists but of Montmartre itself.

"I wrote to Papa, Reverend Mother," Una said gently, "and told him that now I am eighteen the money that Mama left for my education has come to an end. I asked him what he would wish me to do."

"And this is his response!" the Mother Superior said with a somewhat disdainful glance at the telegram lying in front of her.

"It will be nice to be with Papa again," Una said, "and I am too old to be at School."

"I do not like to think of any pupil of mine, and certainly no-one of your age, living in Montmartre," the Mother Superior said.

She looked at Una as she spoke and thought she could say a great deal more on the subject.

It was impossible to think of anyone so beautiful, so attractive as the girl facing her, mixing with artists, dancers and the scum of Paris, who all the world knew inhabited the part that had become a symbol of everything most shocking to the bourgeoisie.

All good Catholics knew that a magnificent Church dedicated to the Sacred Heart had been built on the hill which overlooked Paris and was in fact, in the very centre of the artists' quarter.

But that in itself, was not enough to white-wash the tales of the dancing places, Cabarets and other dubious places of amusement which were a by-word over the whole of Europe.

But this was something which the Mother Superior could not discuss with the girl who faced her.

All she knew was that every instinct within her wished to prevent Una from travelling to Paris to stay with her father.

But Una was not only too old to stay on in the Convent, which was actually a Seminary for the Education of Young Ladies, but also as Una knew herself, with the money left by her mother when she died spent, her education must come to an end.

The Mother Superior made it her policy never to pry into the background of her pupils, but she was well aware that Una's circumstances were rather exceptional.

Apparently her mother, in her will, had stipulated that the whole of her small fortune should be expended on her daughter's education, and a month before she died, she had written herself to the Convent of Notre Dame in Florence asking for particulars.

She had learnt that it was not only the most fashionable place for the daughters of gentle-folk to be educated, but also that the tuition they received there was exceptional in an age when even the richest families considered that the education of their daughters was of little importance.

French girls were in fact better provided for than the English, and the majority of the pupils at the Convent of Notre Dame were French and Italian.

There were a few English girls, but they, because their elementary education had been so inadequate before they arrived, were usually placed in far lower classes for their age, than Una had been.

She was in fact exceptionally intelligent and the Mother Superior wondered now to what use her brain would be put, in the years ahead.

She had always thought that artists were on the whole scruffy in their appearance and without any qualifications except their skill in painting.

She had however, learnt that Una's father did not come into the usual category of painters who frequented Florence and other places rich in artistic treasures.

Julius Thoreau had served in the Grenadier Guards before he had made painting

11

his profession and left England to live in France.

The Mother Superior had never seen any of his pictures, but she had seen an occasional mention of them, not in the artistic reviews which she never read, but in the more conventional and respectable newspapers which occasionally referred to Exhibitions and the new trend in painting.

In the back of the Mother Superior's mind was the idea that Julius Thoreau was just a gentleman enjoying the role of dilettante in the world of art.

She could only hope now, as she looked at his daughter, that he would realise his responsibilities.

He could at least move from Montmartre back to the respectable address outside Paris from which he had written to her in the first place, when it was arranged she should take Una as a pupil.

"I expect, Una," she said now, in her quiet, well-modulated voice, "that your father will now introduce you to Society, and I am sure he will realize that to do so, it would be impossible for you to live in Montmartre."

"When Mama was alive," Una replied, "we were very happy in the little house we had outside Paris. Papa used to paint in the garden, but when he went to Paris Mama and I stayed at home."

"That was of course, very sensible," the Mother Superior approved, "and I am sure your mother would wish you to persuade your father to return to such a life."

Her voice was almost coaxing as she continued:

"After all, I know, Una, that you like the country and might in fact, find it difficult after being here for so long, to acclimatise yourself to living in a great city."

Una did not reply.

She was thinking that it would be, in fact, very exciting to see Paris.

She was sure that her father preferred the gaiety of the most notorious city in the world to the quiet, rather dull existence they had lived in the past.

One of the reasons why her mother had not often gone to Paris, was that they could not afford it.

Even when Una was a child she had learnt that they had to count every penny and that if there was any money available her father would spend it.

When she grew older she learnt that the money in fact, belonged to her mother.

"It was left to me by my grandfather," she explained to Una, "and it was fortunate that he was so kind to me, because otherwise I cannot think what would have happened to us."

Una was nearly fifteen before she learnt that her father had had to leave England and his Regiment because there had been a scandal.

She could never quite understand what had happened except that it concerned something very reprehensible which involved a senior officer.

Whatever the reason, he had been obliged to hand in his resignation rather than face a Court Martial, and he had left his own country in a fury and taken with him the girl to whom he was secretly engaged.

The reason for the secrecy was, Una learnt, that her mother's father had absolutely forbidden the marriage.

When his daughter defied him and ran away with the man he considered 'a bounder' he had cut her out of his life and had no further communication with her.

Una had therefore been born in France and, because her mother talked so wistfully and often so unhappily about England, it always seemed to her to be a Paradise which one day, if she was fortunate, she might visit and be as happy there as her mother had been when she was a girl.

It was strange when all the other girls had

14

so many relations, aunts, uncles, cousins and grandparents, that she should now have only her father.

She thought that as she grew she had missed her mother year by year, even more than she had when she first died.

There were so many things she wanted to talk to her about, so many things she wanted to ask her.

But Mrs Thoreau had died suddenly and unexpectedly, and almost before Una realised what had happened she was in the Convent in Florence and mixing daily with more people than she had met in the last fifteen years.

Because she was so interested in everything that concerned her mother, she studied English, History and Literature more assiduously than any other subjects.

She also made friends with the English girls, and because they came from aristocratic families she learnt a great deal about the English way of living and compared it with that of the French and Italians.

Una was very perceptive in her contacts with people, and the Mother Superior thought, as she looked at her, that there was something sensitive about her and a depth in that sensitivity that was unusual in a young girl.

'I wonder what will happen to her,' the Mother Superior asked herself and aloud she said:

"I hope you will write to me, Una, and tell me exactly what you are doing. Remember I shall always be your friend and ready to help you if it is possible."

"You are very kind, Reverend Mother," Una answered, "and I would like to thank you for all you have taught me, and for all the help you have given me since I have been here."

"Help?" The Mother Superior questioned.

"I realised when I came, how ignorant I was about so many things," Una said simply. "I do not only mean academically."

"I know what you mean, dear," the Mother Superior said.

"I have often thought," Una went on, "how fortunate it was that Mama had chosen this particular place for my education and left the money to pay the fees."

She gave a little sigh.

"I like to think I have not wasted any of my time, but I do realise how much more there is to learn and sometimes I feel very ignorant."

The Mother Superior smiled.

"I can assure you, dear child, that you

16

have learnt and thought much more than most of the girls who pass through my hands, but I am glad you realise there is still a great deal more for you to learn. Most girls of your age think only of getting married."

"I should like to be married one day," Una said, "but in the meantime I hope I shall be able to help Papa."

"I hope so too," the Mother Superior said crisply.

When Una had left her with renewed expressions of gratitude and a genuine note of sadness in her farewells, the Mother Superior had sat for some time without moving.

She was wondering if she should have done more for this strange and unusual child.

Only she, with her vast experience of pupils, knew that while Una had acquired a great deal of academic knowledge, she was completely ignorant of the world outside and particularly of men.

How could she be anything else, considering that she had come to the Convent when she was only fifteen, having, the Mother Superior guessed, led a very sheltered life, and had stayed within its precincts for three years?

But they were, the Mother Superior thought, three vital years in which a girl changed from childhood to stand on the very threshold of womanhood.

"What will become of her?" she asked herself and prayed that Una would find a man who would marry her and, if nothing else, take her away from Montmartre.

The train drew to a standstill at the platform and with a rush the blue-smocked porters came to the carriages crying out:

"Porteur! Porteur!"

Looking through the window Una saw a crown of people on the platform and she wondered how it would be possible to find her father.

Then as Mademoiselle agitatedly collected her charges Una kissed her travelling companions good-bye and promised she would not forget them.

"You must write and tell us what you are doing," Marie-Celeste said, "and perhaps we can meet one day, if Papa lets us come to Paris. It would be fun to visit you in Montmartre, although Mama says it is a place no nice girl would go."

"Come along, Marie-Celeste," Mademoiselle called, descending onto the platform.

Marie-Celeste made a grimace in her direction and kissed Una again.

"Take care of yourself," she said. "I expect you will have a lovely time with all those artists painting pictures of you," and jumped down onto the platform.

Left alone Una collected her hand-bag and her winter coat that was too hot to wear.

The crowds were all moving towards the exit from the platform and Una went with them looking around all the time for a sight of her father.

He was tall and distinguished and looked very English, despite the fact that he sometimes wore rather strange and unconventional clothes which marked him as an artist.

She had nearly reached the end of the platform when she saw her own round-topped leather box being pulled out of the guard's van.

'I had better collect it,' she thought to herself and found a porter who was only too willing to carry it for her.

"Someone meeting you, M'mselle?"

He spoke in the slightly familiar manner which Una knew was not because he was being impertinent but merely because she looked so young that invariably strangers thought she was still a child.

"I think my father will be at the barrier," she replied.

The porter nodded and went ahead, and

she followed him.

There was however, no sign of her father at the barrier, and after waiting for a few minutes, Una thought that perhaps he had forgotten the day she was to arrive.

It was just the sort of thing he would have done in the past.

"Sometimes I think your father has a head like a sieve," her mother had often said half-despairingly, half with amusement.

It was true. He would keep appointments on the wrong day, he would forget anything he had to collect or buy for them in Paris or else bring home entirely the wrong thing because he had forgotten what was originally required.

"I am afraid my father has forgotten me," she said to the porter.

"Don't worry, M'mselle," he replied. "I'll get you a *voiture,* a nice Cocher who'll take you where you want to go."

He spoke in such a protective and fatherly manner that Una smiled at him gratefully.

"That would be very kind of you," she said, and she knew he did choose the cab-driver with care.

She gave him what she thought to be the correct *pourboire.* He thanked her effusively and she thought he looked rather surprised when she gave him the address of her father's Studio in Montmartre.

Once the horse set off from the station Una could only think with delight that she was in Paris.

It seemed to her not three years but a lifetime since she had last been here, and yet now it was so familiar it was like coming home.

The high, grey houses on either side of the streets with their wooden shutters, the crowded Boulevards, the people sitting outside the Cafés at the small marble-topped tables, the pâtisseries, shops and stalls piled high with colourful fruit or great pallid pieces of tripe, were just as she remembered them.

She thought, as they drove along, that she could smell the coffee which never had the same fragrance in Italy.

Now the horse was climbing rather slowly up the hill and high above her, almost as if it blessed her from the sky, was the great white dome of Sacré Cœur.

Una had learned in her studies that it was after the defeat of France at Sedan that a Jesuit had suggested placing France under the protection of the Sacred Heart.

Then the chant had gone up from every Church:

"Save Rome and France in the name of

the Sacred Heart!"

In fact taking advantage of France's enfeebled state Victor Emmanuel had seized the opportunity of taking control of Rome and the Pope declared himself a prisoner in the Vatican.

But the idea of the Church in Paris was an immediate success.

Millions of francs flowed in and it had been the Archbishop of Paris, Cardinal Guibert, who had decided the basilica should be erected in Montmartre.

"It is here," the Prelate cried, "that the Sacred Heart should be enthroned to draw all to itself. On the summit of a hill, a monument to our religious rebirth should be raised."

The Church looked so beautiful now with the sun shining on the white stone that Una thought it was impossible that Montmartre could be as wicked as the girls at School had told her it was.

She was not a Catholic because both her father and mother, being English, were Protestants.

But living in the Convent where nearly all the other pupils were Catholics Una had learnt how important their religion was to them and how deeply it coloured their lives.

She was sure that however sinful

22

Montmartre had been in the past, the Church that by now was nearly completed, would sweep away all that was wrong and diffuse an air of sanctity over the whole place.

The road which led to Montmartre was certainly as steep and as difficult as the ascent into Heaven itself.

The horse was going more and more slowly and now Una could see how different the people looked from those she had passed in the streets and Boulevards below.

Men with velvet jackets and great flowing tics vied with women wearing what almost appeared to be fancy-dress.

They looked strange and at the same time rather exciting and she tried to guess which were errand-girls and boys, laundresses, shop-keepers or poor artisans.

There were some men, Una thought, who were obviously Apaches, and she wondered if the stories she had heard of their fights with knives and pistols in dark alleys were really true.

There were artists sketching on the pavements, or congregating in a Square where the chestnut-trees were in bloom.

The scene was so pretty and the whole place had such an air of gaiety about it that Una drew in her breath with excitement.

It was even more thrilling than she had imagined it would be, and she hoped that her father would allow her to walk round looking at the people and perhaps he would know some of the artists.

She was so busy looking around her that she was surprised when the carriage drew to a standstill outside a tall building that was badly in need of a coat of paint.

It looked drab and had a slight air of desolation which made Una feel apprehensive.

"Here you are, M'mselle!" the Cocher said, shouting at her over his shoulder.

"Thank you," Una replied.

The man climbed down slowly because he was elderly and rather fat, and opened the door of the carriage for her. Then he lifted her trunk down onto the pavement.

She paid him and he asked:

"Shall I carry the trunk in for you, M'mselle?"

"That would be very kind," she answered.

She went ahead through the open door of the house and saw a staircase in a narrow unfurnished hall which looked both dusty and dirty.

"Which number are you going to, M'mselle?" the Cocher enquired.

For the first time Una realised that her father did not own the whole house as she had imagined and it obviously contained several Studios.

She was just about to reply that she had no idea when she saw, stuck to a board, there were three names.

One of them, she saw with relief, was that of her father.

The Cocher saw the board too.

"Well, at least you know who's where," he said.

"My father lives at number three," Una answered.

"That's up the stairs," the Cocher said in a voice of resignation.

Putting her trunk onto his shoulder he climbed up the stairs ahead of her.

They were uncarpeted and creaked ominously under his weight.

On the first floor there was a door on which was inscribed roughly in black paint: "*Julius Thoreau*".

Excitedly Una squeezed past the Cocher on the small landing and knocked.

There was no answer and she opened the door a little tentatively.

She had expected the Studio to look strange but certainly not anything like the large room which was remarkable for its disorder.

There was a sofa, chairs and a table all

mixed up with several easels, a model's throne, a high step-ladder, and propped anywhere were a number of unfinished canvases.

On the walls hung a number of unframed pictures and on the floor were books, boots, dumb-bells, an incredible number of empty bottles and some women's clothes: stockings, scarves, an embroidered Chinese shawl, and an open sunshade.

Una looked about her in bewilderment.

The Cocher put down her trunk.

"Looks as though a good tidying up wouldn't do any harm, M'mselle," he said jovially.

Then before Una could reply he had left her, his heavy footsteps clumping down the stairs.

Una stared around her wondering how anyone could live in such a mess. Then she saw at the far end of the room a narrow wooden staircase and guessed that it must lead to a bedroom.

It passed through her mind that her father might be ill, which would account for his not coming to meet her.

Gingerly she picked her way across the room, dislodging a ball and seeing a piece of beautiful china broken in two lying beside an old boot without laces.

26

She climbed the staircase and found, as she had expected, a small bedroom containing a large divan as a bed and a chest-of-drawers with one leg missing, propped up on books.

There were several broken chairs and the walls were decorated with strange, brilliantly coloured murals of half-naked women.

Una looked at them and felt embarrassed.

As there was no-one in the room, she felt almost as if she was spying on something secret and climbed down the stairs back into the Studio.

There was a large window with a North light and in front of it stood an easel on which she could see a half-finished picture.

Again she manoeuvred her way across the room to look at it.

She recognised that it was her father's work, but he had certainly changed his style a great deal since she had last seen one of his paintings.

He had always used colour in a different manner from other artists.

There had been something unusually beautiful in the manner in which he had brought light into his paintings, giving what he painted a brilliance that made it hold the attention, while the background faded into insignificance.

Una tried to understand what he wished to convey in his paintings, for he had told her that a real artist painted what he felt rather than what he saw with his eyes.

But the picture on the canvas she found entirely incomprehensible, just a mass of swirling colours mingling with each other and without even a recognisable pattern.

'Papa will have to explain this to me,' she thought.

She heard footsteps coming up the stairs and waited with a leap of her heart.

Now she would see her father again. Now everything, which at the moment was rather frightening, would be all right.

The door opened.

Her lips actually moved to exclaim: "Papa!" when she saw it was not her father who stood there, but a middle-aged man, very smartly dressed.

He had a top-hat on the side of his head, a pearl tie-pin in his cravat, and his clothes were fashionably cut, so that with his gold-topped malacca cane, he seemed strangely out of place in the untidy confusion of the Studio.

He walked into the room with an air of authority and for a moment did not see Una standing by the easel.

In fact he walked in the other direction,

towards a picture that hung on the wall just below the steps that led to the bedroom.

Only when he was half-way there did he become conscious of someone else present in the room and turned his head to see Una.

She was standing in the sunshine coming through the window which haloed the childish school-girl's hat she wore on the back of her head and glistened on the gold of her hair as it curled round her oval forehead and the sides of her cheeks.

"Who are you?"

The new-comer's voice was sharp and Una replied, a little nervously:

"I . . . I am waiting for my . . . father."

"Your father?"

"Yes. He told me to come to him in Paris and I thought he would meet me at the station . . . but . . . perhaps I . . . missed him."

"Your father is Julius Thoreau?"

The gentleman spoke slowly, as if he was choosing his words and thinking as he did so.

"Yes. I am his daughter Una."

"And he told you to come to Paris? How long ago?"

"Eight, no nine days ago. He sent me a telegram to the Convent in Florence."

"Nine days! Yes, that is possible."

There was something in the way he spoke

29

which made Una say quickly:

"Is anything . . . wrong? Is Papa . . . ill?"

The gentleman walked towards her.

He had to circumnavigate a chair piled with some broken crockery and a cardboard box which contained a number of black and white ostrich feathers.

Una did not move, but her eyes were very large in her small face.

"What is it? What is wrong?" she asked as the gentleman reached her.

"I am sorry to tell you," he said gently, "that your father was buried yesterday."

"B-buried?"

It was difficult to say the word, then she went on:

"What happened? How is it . . . possible?"

The gentleman's eyes shifted and she had a feeling he was not going to tell her the whole truth.

"Your father had a fall," he said. "It must have affected his heart because when they picked him up, he was dead."

There was no point in telling this child, he told himself, that her father was fighting drunk, that his fall had been down a long flight of stairs and he had broken his neck in the process.

Una clasped her hands together.

"How could . . . anything so . . . terrible

have . . . happened?" she asked, as if she spoke to herself.

"Perhaps in a way, it was a merciful death," the gentleman said consolingly. "Your father did not suffer."

"I am . . . glad of that."

There was a little pause, then she asked:

"Are you a . . . friend of Papa's?"

"I have known your father for many years," the gentleman replied, "and I think he would say I was his friend. In fact, whenever he sold a picture, which was not often, it was I who arranged the sale."

Una gave a little exclamation.

"Now I know who you are!" she said. "You are Monsieur Philippe Dubucheron!"

"That is right. Did your father speak of me?"

"It was Mama who used to say," Una replied, " 'Do tell Monsieur Dubucheron, Julius, that you have a picture finished'."

She did not add that the end of the sentence was always: 'We need the money.'

"I must admit," Monsieur Dubucheron said, "that I had no idea your father had a daughter, nor one, I may say, who is so pretty."

Una looked a little shy at the compliment and he thought that he had never known anything so attractive as the faint colour

31

rising in her cheeks and the way her eyes with their long lashes flickered before his.

They were very unusual eyes, he thought, green with touches of gold in them and they made him think poetically, to his surprise, that they were like the sunshine on a stream.

There was something clear and transparent about the girl that he did not remember seeing in another woman for a very long time, if ever.

Then he told himself he was not familiar with girls from a Convent who were not usually visitors to Julius Thoreau's Studio.

Then suddenly he remembered and it came back to him.

He had come to the Studio ten days ago, or it might only have been nine, and as he reached the top of the stairs a woman had come bursting out through the door, shouting the foul obscenities that were characteristic of the women who frequented Montmartre.

He had entered to find Julius Thoreau at his easel with a paint-brush in his hand. At the same time, he had seen immediately that he was not in a fit state to paint anything.

He was drunk, as Thoreau had been continuously drunk for the last three years since he came to live in Montmartre.

Monsieur Dubucheron had, as it happened, already sold a picture on which Thoreau was engaged.

It had been almost finished two days ago. It annoyed him not to find further work done on it in the meantime and he knew that the woman who had just left, was the model for the figure in the foreground.

"What do you think you are doing, Thoreau?" he asked irritably. "You told me that picture would be ready today. I have a client waiting for it, who is leaving Paris tonight."

"Then he can leave without it!" Julius Thoreau had answered, slurring his words.

"Nothing annoys me more than breaking my promises," Philippe Dubucheron replied, "and what is more, you need the money."

He thought as he spoke, that was unmistakable. Julius Thoreau was wearing a ragged shirt that needed washing and his trousers were smeared with paint.

On his feet were a pair of disreputable felt slippers and it was obvious he had not shaved for twenty-four hours.

He had once been a handsome, distinguished-looking man, but drink had taken its toll of his figure and his looks.

He was bloated and Philippe Dubucheron thought fastidiously, he smelt, as did the whole Studio.

"Very well," he said, "as you have not finished this picture in time, I cannot sell it. Let me know when you wish to see me, because I will never, and this is a promise, Thoreau, sell a picture of yours again until it is completely finished and in my hands."

"I'll finish it, I'll finish it!" Thoreau moaned. "It'll only take me a few hours."

"Without a model?" Philippe Dubucheron enquired.

"Damn the model! Damn the avaricious little harlots! — all they want is money — francs, more francs! That one wouldn't even sit until I paid her!"

"They have to earn their living too!" Philippe Dubucheron said sharply. "Stop being a fool, Thoreau, you cannot finish the picture without a model. Get her back!"

"I wouldn't have her back now, if she went down on her knees!" Julius Thoreau shouted. "I want a model who understands what I'm trying to do — not a piece of wood without a thought in her head except money!"

"You will find no-one who will work for you without payment in Montmartre," Philippe Dubucheron said cynically.

There was silence for a moment. Then suddenly Julius Thoreau had given a loud shout that had made the dealer start.

"I have it!" he exclaimed. "I have the model I want! She won't badger me for money. She'll sit for me because she loves me — do you hear? Because she loves me!"

"I hear you," Philippe Dubucheron said, "although why any woman should love you, God only knows!"

Disgusted he walked towards the door. When he reached it, he turned back to say:

"When you have a picture complete and ready for sale I will come and see you. Otherwise, good-bye!"

He walked down the stairs in a bad temper, angry because he had been fool enough to believe Thoreau when he said he would finish the picture, and disliking more than anything else that he should disappoint a client.

It was not easy to sell pictures at the moment, and if it had not been for other much more lucrative arrangements, Philippe Dubucheron might in fact, have felt the pinch.

But he was too astute and too clever at selling whatever people wanted, to not grow richer and richer year by year.

His silence had made Una feel uneasy.

As if she sensed there was something behind it that she did not know, she asked in a very low voice:

"Can you . . . tell me where . . . Papa is . . . b-buried?"

"Yes, of course," Philippe Dubucheron replied.

Una turned away to stand at the window with her back to him and he knew she was hiding her tears.

"Papa seldom . . . wrote to me," she said, "but when he did . . . he sounded as if everything was going . . . w-well for him. I had no idea . . . he . . . lived like this."

Philippe Dubucheron thought it was not surprising that she was shocked by the appearance of the Studio.

"I expect the woman who cleaned for him has not bothered to come in now that he is dead."

There was silence. Then after a moment Una turned round.

There were tears in her eyes, but he could see that she was making a gallant effort at self-control.

"It seems . . . wrong to ask you at this . . . particular moment," she said, "but does . . . everything here now belong . . . to me?"

"For what it is worth," he replied scornfully.

Then a sudden thought struck him.

"You have some money, I suppose?"

Una shook her head.

"N-no."

"What do you mean — no?" he asked. "All these years when you have not been with your father, you must have had something to live on or been with relatives."

"I have been . . . at school."

"And who paid the school fees?"

"Mama . . . when she died she left everything she possessed to be spent on my education."

That had been a wise move, Philippe Dubucheron thought, otherwise Thoreau would have drunk it away.

"What made you come now to stay with your father?"

"I wrote to Papa to tell him now that I was eighteen the money had all been spent and it was time I left school. Most girls left when they were seventeen."

Philippe Dubucheron calculated that it was this letter that had made Thoreau think of sending for his daughter for an entirely selfish reason.

"Well, what we must arrange," he said briskly, "is, now that your father is dead, for you to go to your relatives in England."

"I . . . cannot do . . . that," Una said quickly.

"Why not?"

"I have no idea who they are or if, in fact, I have any relatives alive. After Mama ran away with Papa, they never spoke to her again."

Philippe Dubucheron stared at her in astonishment.

"Is that true? Are you really telling me that you are completely alone in the world?"

"I am afraid so . . . and I do not know . . . quite what to do."

She looked around the messy, dirty Studio.

"If I were to . . . live here . . . do you think I could . . . get some work?"

"Live here alone?"

"I have . . . nowhere else to go," Una replied.

She thought of the girls she had known at School. They had all gone home to their rich families.

During the three years she had spent in Florence, although her friends, when they were visited by their parents, had sometimes taken her out to luncheon they had never invited her to stay in their homes.

She looked so distressed, so alone, that Philippe Dubucheron surprised himself by saying:

"Do not worry for the moment. I will think of something."

Even as he spoke, he thought he must be deranged.

What would he do with a girl who had come straight from a Convent? Unsophisticated and, he was quite sure, innocent.

She certainly must be that if she thought she could live alone in a place like Montmartre and find employment.

The only employment possible would be —

He stopped.

An idea had come to him, an idea that made him put his hand up to his chin and his eyes narrowed.

"I tell you what we will do," he said slowly. "We will talk this over. But in the meantime, I have an appointment."

He smiled at her reassuringly.

"I will come back, then we will think of a solution to your problems together."

He thought her eyes lit up and she replied:

"It is very kind of you . . . are you quite certain . . . it is no trouble?"

"None at all," he answered, "but I have to leave you now because I am taking that picture of your father's to show to somebody who bought another picture of his a year ago."

He saw the question that Una wanted to ask, without her having to say it.

39

"Of course, the money will be yours, if the sale is concluded — after I have deducted my usual commission."

"Oh, I do hope you sell it!" Una cried. "I do not want to worry you with my problems, but all I have left in my purse is twenty-five francs . . . the journey here was expensive."

"I am sure it was," Philippe Dubucheron replied. "Now I must leave you."

He walked to the picture which hung on the wall and lifted it down from the nail on which it was suspended.

It was a picture of one of the roads in Montmartre in the moonlight.

Patches of light that were characteristic of her father's paintings seemed to make the whole picture stand out in a strange almost sinister fashion that was different from the way any other artist would have seen it.

As Philippe Dubucheron walked towards the door she looked forlorn and lost, standing all alone in the midst of that terrible mêlée of junk that Thoreau had collected around him.

"She is like a snow-drop on a dung-hill," he said to himself and was surprised that he could be so sentimental.

"When I have gone," he said firmly, "shut the door and lock it. You will not let anyone in until I return. Do you understand?"

He saw the surprise in Una's face.

"Do you think . . . people might . . . come here?"

He thought if anyone did so and saw her there, it would be difficult to persuade them to go away. But aloud he said:

"Now it is known that your father is dead, there are always people who will look for pickings to which they are not entitled."

"I . . . understand," Una said.

"Then do as I say. Rest and wait for my return."

"You . . . you will . . . come back?"

It was a child who asked him, a child who was suddenly nervous of being alone in the dark or a thunderstorm.

It made the very level-headed, shrewd procurer both of human beings and anything else that fetched money, feel suddenly protective.

"I will come back," he said with a smile, "and I assure you — I never break a promise! Just be a good girl and do as I told you and everything will be all right."

He smiled at her confidently, and as he went down the stairs, he heard the sound of a key turning in a lock that needed oiling.

The Duke of Wolstanton arrived at his house in Paris in a disagreeable mood.

His Comptroller had wired the previous day, to say he was on his way, but even at such short notice everything was in readiness for him.

It would have been difficult to find fault with the array of flunkeys in the Wolstanton livery, the flowers which decorated the Salon, and the pristine cleanliness which made the whole house seem polished like the silver that stood on the Dining-Room table.

The Duke however, scowled as he was greeted by the Clerk of the Chambers and making only a monosyllabic reply, walked into the Salon and threw himself down in a comfortable chair.

Two flunkeys hurried to his side with a bottle of champagne cooled to exactly the right temperature and the Duke taking a glass from the gold salver, sipped it without enthusiasm.

He had left London on an impulse because he had suddenly made one of those momentous decisions in his life that only he could do, with a ruthlessness and a lack of consideration for other people's feelings which was inexcusable.

Or rather it would have been inexcusable in any other man.

But the Duke of Wolstanton was too important, too rich and too attractive for anyone to be prepared to take umbrage for any length of time, at anything he did.

He was however, quite certain that at this moment, Rose Caversham was biting her finger-nails with fury and he would doubtless, in tomorrow's post, receive several pages of protest written when her anger was flaring.

Lady Rose Caversham was noted for a temper that made people wonder what had hit them, but which usually subsided as quickly as it arose.

He could hardly remember now what had started the quarrel, but it ended as was inevitable, with Rose declaring that he was the most selfish man alive, that he had ruined her reputation, and the only way in which he could make reparation was to marry her immediately.

This was an old argument which the Duke had always managed to side-track extremely adroitly on a great many other occasions.

He had supposed for some time that sooner or later he would marry Rose.

After all, he had to marry somebody and have an heir to take over the Wolstanton estates which were the largest in the British Isles, but he had every intention of choosing the time and place when he was ready, and not before.

He was well aware that he and Rose were talked about, but then any woman that he squired, if even for one evening, became immediately the victim of not only the social gossips, but also of the yellow press.

There was nothing reporters enjoyed more, than speculating who the Duke of Wolstanton would marry and how soon the nuptials would take place.

The quarrel between herself and Rose might, in fact, have been made up with kisses in the inevitable manner of such wordy battles, had not Rose, in losing her temper, not only reproached the Duke for not marrying her, but had threatened him.

This was something he would not tolerate from anyone, and he knew as Rose shrieked at him, that for once she had gone too far.

He walked out of her bedroom slamming the door behind him, and driving back home in his carriage, drawn by two tired horses and driven by a tired coachman with a yawning footman beside him, had decided he would leave London.

The Duke owned houses in various parts of the world which were always ready for him to visit at a moment's notice.

There was a large Villa in the South of

France, another in Tangier; and a Castle in Scotland, a Hunting-Lodge in Leicester-shire and a Mansion in Ireland, where he had not been for the past five years.

He had chosen Paris simply because he thought to learn of it would annoy Rose more than any of the others, because she would be jealous of the very amusing times he spent with the notorious *demi-mondaines* in that delightful city.

The Prince of Wales had, in fact, teased Rose only a few weeks ago, when he said:

"I am thinking of taking Blaze with me the next time I visit Paris. I enjoy myself very much *en garçon*, but Blaze tells me that I am missing some very alluring haunts in which it is not considered respectable for me to be seen."

"If Blaze goes to Paris, Sir, then I shall go with him!" Rose had said, with a meaningful glance at the Duke.

"That would indeed be taking 'coals to Newcastle'!" the Prince of Wales had re-torted, then laughed heartily at his own joke.

The Duke had never had any intention of taking Rose with him to Paris, but he knew she would understand exactly why he had chosen to go there when he left England without their making up their quarrel.

The Duke of Wolstanton was in fact, a very intelligent man, but because he found time heavy on his hands, he spent a great deal of it, like the majority of his contemporaries, making love to attractive women without really considering if there was any alternative.

Life had always been too easy for the Duke: together with the fact that he was so rich and of such social consequence, it had really been unnecessary that he should also be so handsome.

Women were bowled over at the sight of him, and by the time he had left Oxford, he was aware that they were ready to fall into his arms even before he knew their Christian names.

It was, he had thought to himself once, like eating too much *pâté de foie gras*. Taken occasionally, it was delicious, but a surfeit of it became boring.

It was because he was surfeited too easily with the women who clustered round him wherever he went and whatever he was doing that the Duke had managed so far, by sheer strength of will to remain unmarried.

He was nearly thirty-five and all his friends had succumbed a long time ago, to the pressure of their parents and the women who were determined to trap them into being led meekly up the aisle.

But that did not prevent them from indulging, like the Prince of Wales, in a continuous stream of love-affairs, while their wives either pretended ignorance or became immune.

Sometimes when the Duke was alone, which was not often, he wondered if his life in the years ahead held anything but a monotonous series of women, each lovely, alluring, seductive, fascinating, passing through his arms and his bed and from there into oblivion.

It was a depressing thought which made him move from one of his houses to another. But his followers always arrived post-haste within a few hours of his attempt to find solitude.

"I sometimes feel like a hunted stag," he said once, to one of his friends.

"Doubtless a stag, but a Royal or an Imperial," his friend replied and the Duke had to laugh.

Now he told himself he would enjoy Paris without the usual crowd of hangers-on who ate his food and drank his wine and expected him to accommodate them in the style to which they had become accustomed, wherever he might be.

47

As his Comptroller came into the Salon, he put down his glass of champagne and said:

"You quite understand, Beaumont, that I want nobody to stay, and I want no arrangements made for me."

"Of course, Your Grace," Mr Beaumont replied.

He had not only controlled the Duke's households, but also befriended the Duke himself, over many years.

The Duke said now, half-angrily:

"Dammit, Beaumont, I know you are thinking that this mood will not last more than twenty-four hours, but you are mistaken!"

"I hope I am," Mr Beaumont answered.

"Why should you say that?" the Duke asked curiously.

"Because I think a change of environment is just what you need at the moment."

"And you think Paris will provide that?"

"If you are not cluttered by the usual chorus who echo everything you say, and what they think you think."

The Duke laughed.

For the first time since he had left London, it was a genuine sound of amusement.

"I employ you as a Comptroller, not as a

Doctor," he said. "What is your prescription?"

"I should imagine a little of the Moulin Rouge, a soupçon of the Théâtre des Variétés, and of course, some new and entrancing voice, preferably with a French accent, to tell you how wonderful you are."

The Duke laughed again, then he said:

"You are sacked! I cannot employ anyone who treats me with so little respect."

"I respect you enough to want you to be happy," Mr Beaumont said.

"And what is happiness?" the Duke asked.

"I suppose only each of us can answer that for ourselves," Mr Beaumont replied, "but I can tell you one thing it is not — and that is being cynical!"

"Are you suggesting that I am cynical?"

"I have watched you getting more and more cynical these past five years. I have watched you becoming blasé and I have watched you finding little pleasure in anything except perhaps your horses, and I think it is a pity."

"That is certainly straight-speaking," the Duke said ruefully.

"It is something I have wanted to say for a long time," Mr Beaumont replied, "and quite frankly, and you may hate me for saying this, I think you are wasting your life."

The Duke looked startled and sat up in his chair.

"Do you mean that?"

"I would hardly say it otherwise."

"No, I do not think you would," the Duke answered.

He waited for a moment, then he said:

"I suppose in some ways I have been closer to you, Beaumont, than anyone else in my whole life. I hated my father. I have a great number of friends, but I have never wanted to be particularly intimate with them. I suppose you are the only man to whom I speak the truth and from whom I expect to hear it."

"Thank you," Mr Beaumont said. "I am five years older than you, but I think on the whole, I enjoy myself a great deal more than you, in spite of all your possessions and the assets you seldom consider."

"What are they?" the Duke asked curiously.

"Your brains, for one thing," Mr Beaumont replied.

The Duke rose from his chair and walked across the room.

He stood looking out at the beautifully kept formal garden which stood at the back of the house in the Rue du Faubourg St Honoré.

"This brain business," he said after a moment. "Do you really use a brain or do you only need it to acquire money? I have all the money I can possibly want, not only in my lifetime, but in half-a-dozen others. Then what use is it to me, except to make me discontented?"

"That is the most encouraging thing I have ever heard you say," Mr Beaumont remarked.

"What the devil do you mean by that?" the Duke asked.

"Do you not remember that Napoleon spoke of 'divine discontent? That is what we all need — discontent': with conditions they are not perfect; with people who are not up to what is required of them — and with yourself, because you cannot reach your highest aspirations."

"Good God!" the Duke exclaimed. "I had no idea you felt like this. Why have you not told me before?"

Mr Beaumont smiled.

"I thought of it, but there did not seem to be an opportunity and you did not ask me."

He looked at the Duke and his eyes were very understanding.

"I have a feeling, although I may be wrong,

that you have reached a cross-roads in your life. It is up to you which way you take."

"That sounds slightly dramatic," the Duke said. "The only thing is, I have not the slightest idea which way to go, whether I should turn left or right, is quite immaterial."

"I doubt it," Mr Beaumont answered. "In the years to come, you will look back at this moment and remember I told you you had reached a cross-roads."

"Well, I thought I was doing something unusual in coming to Paris in such a hurry," the Duke said, "but I had no idea I was letting myself in for a lot of sermonising from you!"

"You can always ignore it," Mr Beaumont said, "and that, I suspect is exactly what you will do."

"Go away!" the Duke shouted. "Go away and leave me to my bad temper and depression. You make things worse, much worse than I even imagined them to be!"

"I am delighted," Mr Beaumont said. "And now, would you like to tell me what theatre seats I should book for you and where you would like to dine tonight?"

As he finished speaking, the door opened and a servant announced:

"Monsieur Philippe Dubucheron, Your Grace!"

2

As soon as Philippe Dubucheron entered the room, Mr Beaumont left it.

He realised that he had not had time to give the servants the Duke's instructions that he would see nobody, and His Grace's solitude had therefore been interrupted.

Dubucheron was the type of hanger-on whom Mr Beaumont most disliked, although he told himself there was some excuse for the French dealer because he had something to sell.

At the same time, he thought that the manner in which he was prepared to procure women for his patrons, to introduce them to the more seamy Cabarets and every other low type of entertainment in Paris, was extremely undesirable.

The Duke was old enough to look after himself.

At the same time, men like Dubucheron only pandered to the tastes that Mr Beaumont deplored and, he was quite certain, added to the Duke's air of cynicism.

He had also surprised himself in the way he had been so out-spoken.

But he genuinely believed that the Duke was drifting in a manner which did no credit to his personality and character and certainly damaged his reputation.

Mr Beaumont admired the man he served for his many fine qualities and, unlike all the other people who surrounded the Duke, was not in the least impressed by his wealth and possessions.

He had actually, although the Duke had no idea of it, been offered several very interesting posts in the City since he had become the Duke's Comptroller.

They would have given him the opportunity of making much more money than the salary he earned from the Duke and might have led later, to a seat in Parliament, for which he was actually extremely well fitted.

But he had stayed with the Duke because he knew that if he were not there, the hangers-on who toadied to him, who had their hands permanently in his pockets, and who were doing their best to spoil him as an individual, would have had a field-day.

Mr Beaumont was a man of very high principles and he had been brought up in a family where duty came first.

He had long decided that his duty lay in

looking after the Duke of Wolstanton and if possible saving him from himself.

He was not the slightest bit priggish or sanctimonious about the Duke's way of life.

A young man, especially with the Duke's advantages, was expected to 'sow his wild oats' and take advantage of whatever favours the fair sex were prepared to grant him.

But the Duke was no longer as young as he had been when Mr Beaumont first moved into his household in Park Lane. He was nearly thirty-five and approaching the prime of his life.

Mr Beaumont knew better than anyone else that it was essential for the Duke to marry, and to marry the right type of woman.

He had therefore secretly been delighted when Lady Rose's ungovernable temper had sent the Duke posting, at a moment's notice, to Paris to get away from her.

Mr Beaumont disliked Lady Rose, as he had disliked most of the women who had tried desperately, by every means in their power, to marry the Duke in the last few years.

Yet he sometimes asked himself almost as cynically as his master, what was the alternative.

The women whom the Duke met in the 'Marlborough House Set' hosted by the Prince of Wales, or whom he himself invited to Wolstanton House, were all sophisticated, glittering, scintillating Social Queens.

They tried to trap a man they desired with all the skill and expertise of an accomplished poacher.

Each time a new woman appeared on the Duke's horizon, Mr Beaumont found himself groaning and when he had made her acquaintance sending up a prayer in his heart which was nearly always the same:

"Not this one, dear God, not this one!"

He walked to his office which was an extremely comfortable room situated on the ground floor.

From here, like a spider spinning its web, he made the wheels of the house run so smoothly that the Duke never had the slightest idea how much was involved in providing for his comfort.

Mr Beaumont sat down at his desk and as he did so, he wondered how long it would be before the Duke sent for him to write a cheque for the picture which Dubucheron had carried in his hand.

The Duke was, at that moment, inspecting the picture.

"How did you know I was here?" the Duke had asked first, as Philippe Dubucheron approached him with an ingratiating smile that signified he was expecting to make a good sale.

"It was in the luncheon time edition of *Le Jour*," Philippe Dubucheron replied.

The Duke made a sound of annoyance.

"I have always suspected that one of the servants here gives out information about me to the newspapers. Now I am sure of it! No-one knew I was coming to Paris until this morning when the household learnt the time of my arrival."

"It is delightful to see Your Grace," Philippe Dubucheron said hastily, "and I have something which I think will interest you."

"I might have guessed it!" the Duke exclaimed. "What is it?"

"The last picture painted by Julius Thoreau before he died."

That was untrue, as the picture had been painted nearly two years previously, before Thoreau began drinking so heavily, but Dubucheron achieved the effect he desired.

"Dead? I had no idea that Thoreau was dead," the Duke exclaimed.

"He died a week ago from the usual disease which carries off the best artists we have."

"Absinthe?" the Duke queried.

"Exactly!"

As Dubucheron spoke, he undid the wrapping which covered the picture he had taken from Julius Thoreau's Studio.

He held it up and as he did so, he thought it was actually one of the best paintings he had ever done.

Strangely enough he had not been able to find a buyer for it, although he had tried several different Americans, and one Italian.

He set it down on a sofa where it faced the light and the Duke stood back to examine it, noting the strange effect of light in the rather sordid street.

"I do not know what it is," he said, almost to himself, "but Thoreau's pictures have a strange effect on me. They make me feel they are telling me something, if only I could understand what it is."

Dubucheron did not answer.

He was a clever enough businessman not to impose his own ideas on his clients, unless of course, it concerned the price.

"How much are you asking for it?"

It was the conventional question and the Duke spoke absent-mindedly, as if he was thinking of something else.

Dubucheron named a figure which was

double what he expected to get and the Duke did not accept nor refuse. He only went on looking at the picture.

Then as if he forced his attention away from it, he said:

"What are the latest amusements in Paris? Is there a new star in the theatrical firmament?"

"I have someone I think you would like to meet," Dubucheron answered, "if only as an experience."

"What do you mean by that?"

"I am speaking of Yvette Joyant. She is a dancer of some merit, but her personality is more exceptional than her talent."

"I do not seem to know the name."

"She has not been performing lately. She has been mistress of the Duc d'Almare, but he has just left her and she is now what the theatrical profession call 'resting'."

The Duke smiled.

"What you are suggesting, Dubucheron, is that I might put in a bid which would doubtless be accepted."

"She would certainly amuse you while you are here," Dubucheron answered, "although perhaps I should warn you, that she is spoken of as the most seductively evil woman who has ever graced the ranks of her profession."

"What you are really offering me is a challenge," the Duke said. "If I find her as entertaining as you suggest, I shall have to admit that I am an old dog who is prepared to learn new tricks. If, however, I am bored, then I am sure you will make certain that you have nothing to lose."

Philippe Dubucheron bowed obsequiously.

"Your Grace always enjoys pulling my leg," he said, "but if you find Mademoiselle Yvette not to your liking, then I have another suggestion to make."

"What is that?"

"You might like to meet Thoreau's daughter."

"His daughter!" the Duke exclaimed. "Is she an artist like her father?"

"No," Philippe Dubucheron replied, "she is very young, very innocent, and has just arrived in Paris to find herself an orphan and stranded without any money."

"Are you asking me to be a philanthropist?" the Duke enquired. "I imagine that what I pay you for this picture will help to keep her in comfort for a week or so."

"But of course," Philippe Dubucheron replied, "I was just thinking myself that the two women are in such sharp contrast that I might be offering you the choice of descending into

60

Hell or ascending into Heaven."

He thought to himself that he had appraised the situation rather cleverly.

He did not realise that the Duke was remembering that only a few minutes earlier Mr Beaumont had told him that he stood at a cross-roads.

"I thought you offered me a challenge, Dubucheron," he remarked, "but I see instead, it is a conundrum."

"The choice is yours," Philippe Dubucheron said quickly. "As you say, the sale of her father's picture will obviously help the situation as far as Miss Thoreau is concerned, but she is too innocent and too inexperienced, to be left alone in Paris."

"I quite understand that you are trying to intrigue me," the Duke said, "but you must have forgotten I had an experience once before, of your idea of innocence. Do you not remember Mimi Fénon?"

Philippe Dubucheron laughed.

"Of course, Your Grace. I confess that at the time, I was deceived by a very experienced and very astute little actress, but you must admit I had some justification. She certainly looked as innocent as she pretended to be."

"She cost me a sum of money which made even Beaumont gasp!" the Duke said. "But on looking back, I think the lesson it taught me was worth it."

"And what was that?" Dubucheron asked, as if he knew it was expected of him.

"Never to trust a woman who tells you she has not a penny in her purse, and nowhere to sleep the night."

Philippe Dubucheron threw out his arms in an expressive gesture.

"Very well, Your Grace, you win!" he said. "Shall I tell Yvette Joyant that you will take her out to dinner? You may well leave the rest of the evening to her."

"I suppose I must trust to your judgement," the Duke said. "You have only failed me once, Dubucheron, and I think I must be fair in saying that Mimi Fénon was not exactly a failure. It was only when I unwrapped the parcel, I found its content were not what I expected."

Dubucheron threw back his head in an almost exaggerated expression of mirth.

"Well phrased, Your Grace!" he exclaimed. "It is not surprising that you are described as the greatest wit in England to set foot in Paris."

It was blatant flattery and the Duke accepted it as his right.

Philippe Dubucheron took a long look at the picture on the sofa which recalled the

Duke's attention to what was obviously expected.

"Stop in at Mr Beaumont's office as you leave," he said, "and ask him for a cheque."

"Thank you, Your Grace, and I was just wondering," Philippe Dubucheron said, "if Thoreau has left any other pictures in his Studio, whether you would like to see them."

"Why not?" the Duke enquired. "I like Thoreau's work and it is a pity he is dead. He could not have been very old."

"About forty-five, Your Grace."

"There would have been a lot of work still left in him had he not succumbed to that damned poison. I was hearing, the other day, from one of your Generals in London, of the damage it has done in the Army."

"It is a curse for the whole of France," Philippe Dubucheron agreed, "and, as Your Grace has said, it is a pity Thoreau had to die so young."

He thought as he spoke, that if Thoreau had lived, the pictures he had recently been producing would not have fetched a *sou* from any connoisseur.

He was, at the same time, turning over in his mind whether there was anything left that had escaped his notice of Thoreau's earlier works.

He decided he would hurry back to the Studio and look the canvasses over that were on the floor, and perhaps there would be some in the bedroom or hidden away in the dirty little hole that Thoreau called a kitchen.

"I will call tomorrow, Your Grace," he said. "In the meantime, may I wish you a very pleasant evening with the delectable Yvette? I will leave her address with Mr Beaumont."

Philippe Dubucheron's hand was actually on the doorhandle when the Duke, who was still looking at the picture on the sofa, said:

"Wait!"

The Frenchman stopped and turned his head tentatively.

"I have an idea," the Duke said. "Why should I meet Mademoiselle Yvette in this informal manner without an introduction?"

"Introduction, Your Grace?" Dubucheron asked in a puzzled voice.

"It is just a suggestion," the Duke said, "but why do you not dine with me, Dubucheron, and Thoreau's daughter could make up the foursome."

The Duke's lips twisted in a smile as he added:

"I can then, while both ladies are with me, make my choice of direction, as you so concisely put it: of descending into Hell or ascending into heaven."

For a moment Philippe Dubucheron was too astonished to reply.

In all the years he had known the Duke, he had never been invited to dine with him. In fact, their acquaintance had always been a purely business-like relationship.

Now he felt he could not have understood the Duke aright, but before he could speak, the Duke went on:

"We will dine here. It will give me a chance to see the ladies in more comfortable circumstances, and so I suggest you bring them both to meet me at eight o'clock."

"It will be an honour and a privilege, Your Grace," Philippe Dubucheron said, "and I promise you that, if nothing else, your first evening in Paris will evoke a piquancy that is original . . ."

He paused for a moment to add:

". . . like the Chinese sweet and sour sauce!"

He did not wait for the Duke's reply but went from the room with a smile on his face, which infuriated Mr Beaumont when he saw it.

The sun had begun to sink and the shadows in the untidy Studio had begun to deepen while Una waited for Monsieur Dubucheron to return.

When he left she had at first, started to try to tidy some of the jumble which made it almost impossible to move about the large room, but after a while she gave it up.

Everything was so dusty and dirty, and although she felt quite tired with the exertion, she did not seem to have made any difference to the general confusion.

She found what she supposed was the kitchen and washed her hands in the sink, but she was appalled by the dirt and the congealed grease where food had been cooked.

The window was filthy and let in so little light that it was almost impossible to see what she was doing.

When she went back into the Studio she looked again at the picture her father had been painting before he died and tried to understand it.

Although she had loved his pictures in the past, this was so incomprehensible that she had the uncomfortable feeling that his mind might have been deranged while he painted it.

She thought she ought to feel absolutely grief-stricken because her father was dead.

But somehow, sitting in his ghastly Studio

she felt she had lost someone she did not know; someone who was certainly not the handsome, dashing father she had loved when her mother was alive.

There was an enormous number of empty wine bottles on the floor, on the table, and arranged like skittles along the window-sill, which posed a question she did not wish to answer.

She remembered in the past, her mother saying with a sigh:

"I wish your father would not drink so much when he goes to Paris. He always comes home looking so ill. Drink has never agreed with him."

"He does not drink at home, Mama," she recalled saying.

"For the simple reason that we cannot afford it, dearest," her mother had answered, "but when Papa is with his friends he likes to do as they do."

Una could only wonder now what sort of friends her father had known since he had come to live in Montmartre — friends who had encouraged him to drink even though it made him ill.

Friends who were perhaps responsible for the whirling and inexplicable colours that twisted and turned over the canvas with no rhyme or reason to them.

It was impossible not to think of her own situation at the moment. What was she to do?

If Monsieur Dubucheron sold the picture, she would at least have a little money which would give her time to look around and find somewhere to live and get a job of some sort.

The odd thing was that all the years she had spent being educated had not given her a saleable talent.

"I can play the piano a little," Una told herself, "I can paint, but only in a very amateurish way. I can sew and that is about all! I have to think of something . . . I have to!"

She spoke aloud almost despairingly and thought her voice sounded like that of a ghost echoing round the big Studio.

Finally she decided that perhaps if she applied at some Schools they might require a mistress who could teach English or at least look after smaller children.

Then as she thought of it, and it seemed a sensible idea, she remembered how very young she looked and how young, in fact, she was in years.

All the mistresses in the Convent had been Nuns who came in to teach special subjects and were middle-aged women, chosen, Una felt sure, because they had the authority to keep the pupils in order and make them learn.

She rose from the chair in which she had been sitting to see if she could find a mirror in which she could look at her reflection.

It had not, of course, altered since she had seen her reflection when arranging her hair in the train.

But then she had been looking at herself to see if she looked attractive enough to please her father, not because she required a presence and an authority which would make parents and school-teachers trust her with young children.

The only mirror in the place she found was upstairs in her father's bedroom.

It stood on the chest-of-drawers and was cracked across the centre.

She looked at herself for a long time, then took off her hat wondering if it was the almost childish creation on the back of her head, which made her look so very young and, as it happened, so very frightened.

The half-naked women depicted on the walls seemed to stare at her with contempt and Una hurried down the rickety stairs back to the Studio.

Now her imagination began to frighten her even more.

Supposing Monsieur Dubucheron forgot

about her? Suppose he never came back? How long should she stay here waiting for him, and if she decided to leave, where would she go?

She began to feel hungry, but he had said she was not to leave the Studio or let anyone into it.

"What am I to do?"

The question seemed almost to be shouted at her from the pictures on the walls.

Because she thought they made her even more frightened, she walked to the window.

She looked up at the sky and prayed.

Ever since her mother had died she had found herself, when she said her prayers, sometimes saying them to God, sometimes to her mother.

She often thought foolishly that God was too busy to hear her, but her mother would always be listening.

It was the thought of her mother that brought the tears to Una's eyes.

"Oh, Mama," she said, "help me. What shall I do? Where shall I go? I am so alone."

It was as she said the last words, that she heard footsteps coming up the stairs and hastily wiped away the tears.

She hoped it was Monsieur Dubucheron, but if it was not, she wondered what she should do if somebody finding the door locked, tried to force it open.

Then there was a knock and a voice said:

"Are you there, Mademoiselle? It is I — Philippe Dubucheron!"

With a little cry of thankfulness because she was so glad he had come, Una ran across the room and unlocked the door.

"Monsieur, you are back!" she cried.

She stated the obvious because she was so pleased to see him.

Monsieur Dubucheron seemed larger, smarter and more overpowering than she had remembered.

"Yes, I am back, Mademoiselle," he said, "and I have good news for you."

"Good news?"

"Yes. I have sold your father's picture and have quite a considerable amount of francs to give you tomorrow, when I cash my client's cheque."

Una clasped her hands together.

"Oh, thank you, Monsieur Dubucheron. I am so grateful and you are very kind."

"I have something else to tell you," he said. "My client, who is an admirer of your father's painting, has invited you to dine with him tonight."

"Was he a friend of Papa's?" Una asked.

Philippe Dubucheron shook his head.

"Not a friend," he replied. "He bought a

picture of your father's a year ago and he is delighted with the one I took to him just now."

"I am glad! So very glad!" Una cried. "It was kind of him to ask me to dinner . . . but I am sure you suggested it, Monsieur."

"That is very perceptive of you, my dear. As a matter of fact, I did!" Monsieur Dubucheron replied. "We are dining at His Grace's house on the Rue du Faubourg St Honoré at eight o'clock."

He looked at her, then enquired:

"You have an evening gown with you?"

"Yes," Una replied. "It is in my trunk."

She pointed, as she spoke, to the round-topped leather trunk which stood just inside the door where the Cocher had left it.

Monsieur Dubucheron looked around the Studio.

"I can hardly expect you to change here," he said, "and I doubt if there is any water in which you can wash."

"There is only a tap in the very dirty kitchen."

"I will take you somewhere where you can change," he said. "Come with me now, and I will send my coachman up to collect your trunk."

Hastily Una picked up her hat from where she had laid it and put it on her head. Her overcoat was lying on a chair and beside it, with her gloves, was a little leather handbag which contained all the money she possessed in the world.

She picked them up and turned her face to Philippe Dubucheron with an anxious expression in her large eyes.

"I shall have to find somewhere to sleep, Monsieur."

"Yes, I know," Philippe Dubucheron replied, "but I think for the moment, we will leave that in the lap of the gods."

He saw Una look puzzled. Then without making any further explanations he preceded her down the stairway.

As he had no desire to let her do anything that might seem strange or reprehensible, at least until the Duke had seen her, Philippe Dubucheron did not take her back to his own apartment.

It would in fact, have been the easiest thing to do.

He lived in considerable luxury in a quiet road near the Opéra and employed a couple of servants who cooked and looked after him in a manner that was the continual envy of his friends.

But for Una to say, however innocently, that she had changed for dinner in an apartment belonging to a man, would be, he thought, to start her off on the wrong foot.

Philippe Dubucheron was adept at planning every detail of one of his sales.

Accordingly he conveyed Una in his carriage to a small, but fashionable Art Gallery in which he had a fifty-fifty interest which was just off the Rue de la Paix.

He seldom took his more distinguished or more prosperous clients there, finding it far easier to convince them of what they should buy when he showed them one or two pictures in their own homes.

The majority of people who came to Paris were, Philippe Dubucheron found, extremely ignorant and bought a picture merely because they wanted to take home something which came from the gay city.

It was easy to mesmerise them into accepting what he assured them was a bargain and 'the chance of a lifetime' when they were not bemused by a large choice.

Philippe Dubucheron's father was an extremely astute man who had told him, when he was quite small that most people had a very limited vision and even more limited minds.

"Never confuse a client, my dear Philippe. Decide what you want him to do and make him believe that what he thinks is his own idea, when actually it is yours."

It was a principle that had made Philippe Dubucheron the most important and certainly the most successful Art Dealer in Paris.

Yet, because he had an original mind, he found it very boring to confine himself entirely to pictures.

The men he got to know in the course of business, were noblemen from every part of Europe and he found they were not only interested in art, but in anything that appealed to their senses.

It was a game he played with himself and gave him a satisfaction which was as pleasant as backing a theatrical show and finding it a success, that he should provide every man with what he most desired.

His clients therefore ranged from Kings and Rulers, from Egyptian Potentates and German Princes, to the English who came to Paris merely for amusement.

Philippe Dubucheron grew to know them all, and because he served them well, they always returned to him, confident that he would supply their needs, whatever they might be.

The Picture Gallery in which he was interested established him in the right category from a French point of view.

"Who is Dubucheron?" a stranger would

ask, only to be told immediately:

"The Art Dealer. He has a Gallery in the Rue de la Cambon."

"Labels are important in my trade," Philippe Dubucheron often thought.

His own label was respectable enough to satisfy the most carping critic and there were quite a number of them.

The Art Gallery was, of course, shut by this time of night, but he opened it with a key he carried with him and switching on the lights, invited Una to follow him inside.

"I have an office at the end of the Gallery," he said, "and there is also a small washing-place attached to it. There are plenty of mirrors in which you can arrange your hair."

Una wanted to stop and look at the pictures in the Gallery itself, but Philippe Dubucheron hurried her into the office.

It was luxuriously furnished with a thick carpet on the floor and a somewhat pretentious desk on the period of Louis XIV.

His coachman carried in her trunk and on Monsieur's orders, undid the straps.

"It is very kind of you to let me come here," Una said.

Philippe Dubucheron drew out an expensive gold watch from the pocket of his waistcoat.

"It is now just after seven o'clock," he said. "I will call for you at exactly ten minutes to eight. Please be ready, and have your trunk packed so that it can come with you."

"That gives me plenty of time," she answered with a smile.

"I want you to look your very best tonight," Philippe Dubucheron said. "I hardly need tell you that it is an honour that the Duke should have invited you to dine with him, and I hope you will make yourself as charming as possible. I would not like him to be disappointed in your father's daughter."

"No, of course not," she answered, "and he must be a very nice man to have bought two of Papa's pictures."

"He is a very nice man," Philippe Dubucheron repeated rather heavily.

Then looking once again at his watch he went from the office closing the door behind him.

It was then that Una thought how strange and unexpected everything had turned out to be.

She had never thought when she left Florence, that instead of being with her father when she lived in Paris, she would be dining with an English Duke and changing her clothes in a Picture Gallery.

"The girls will never believe me when I tell them about it," she said to herself.

Then she remembered that it was very unlikely she would ever have a chance of telling them anything about her life.

It was not because she did not make friends or because they did not like her.

She was not being conceited when she knew that she was one of the most popular girls in the School.

It was just that the fathers and mothers of her friends were all foreigners who had very strict ideas about whom their children should or should not know.

Artists, however gifted they might be, were not accepted socially and Una had soon learnt that it was unlikely, once she had left School, that she would ever see any of her friends again.

It was something she knew she must accept sensibly without complaining.

'At least Mama will know,' she thought to herself, as she started to take off the gown in which she had travelled, 'and Mama will be pleased that he is English.'

Una could remember many times when her mother had talked not only about England, but about the English people.

To her, they would always be preferable in every way to the French, even though the people in the small village where they lived had been fond of the Thoreaus and had made them feel welcome.

But Una's mother would talk of hunting over the English countryside in the winter, of boating and playing tennis in the summer, of attending Balls at which the ladies glittered in jewelled tiaras and the men wore decorations because Royalty was present.

She had described to Una the Drawing-Room at Buckingham Palace in which she had made her curtsey to Queen Victoria and how charming the Prince of Wales had been, when he had danced with her once at a Hunt Ball.

It all sounded so entrancing that Una would often find herself dreaming about England.

She would forget that outside the Convent windows the tall cypress trees were silhouetted against the sky, in the conventional Florentine landscape which was repeated a hundred times in the pictures in the Uffizi Gallery.

"If I dress quickly," she told herself now, "I shall be able to look at the pictures before we leave."

But actually dressing took longer than she had anticipated.

First of all she had to shake the creases

out of her evening-gown which she realised when she had taken it out, was not really smart enough to dine with a Duke.

She had bought what clothes she required in Florence and the Mother Superior had paid for them out of the money her mother had left for her education.

They were very plain, school-girls' clothes, well-cut, and of pricey material, but at the same time, demure young girls' gowns that had made Una look very youthful, however much older she actually grew in years.

Her best gown was white with a little frill of lace around the neck and around the three-quarter sleeves.

It accentuated her tiny waist and the soft immature curves of her breasts, but she thought a little apprehensively that perhaps Monsieur Dubucheron would not think she was smart enough and would be ashamed to introduce her to the Duke.

Because she was worried, she took extra care in arranging her hair.

It was very soft and fair and she had no idea what was the fashionable coiffure in Paris.

She finally arranged it as she had worn it at the Convent, swept back from her forehead, seeming to halo her small face and coiled in a bun at the nape of her neck.

It was, although she did not realise it, a style which had become *le dernier cri* on the other side of the Atlantic because of Dana Charles Gibson's brilliant drawings of American beauties.

To Una it was just a style which her hair seemed to fall into naturally and again she hoped that Monsieur Dubucheron would not think it too simple.

Worrying about herself, and having taken so long in washing in the elaborately fitted china basin encased in heavy mahogany, she only just had time to pack the clothes she had worn into her trunk before the door of the office opened and Monsieur Dubucheron reappeared.

"You are ready?"

She thought that his eyes looked her over from top to toe and she felt embarrassed by his scrutiny and, at the same time, anxious in case he should find fault.

"You look charming!" he smiled, "and now we must not be late, so come along!"

The coachman appeared and picked up her trunk.

Then as Una, slipping a plain woollen shawl over her shoulders reached the carriage, with Monsieur Dubucheron, she realised there was someone else inside.

She stepped in and as Monsieur Dubucheron followed her and he sat down on the small seat with his back to the horses, he said:

"Yvette, let me introduce Miss Una Thoreau — Mademoiselle Yvette Joyant!"

"What is all this about, Philippe?" a deep voice asked from a corner of the carriage.

"I told you that Miss Thoreau will make a four at dinner. I think afterwards, we may go our separate ways, but I am not sure."

"I am quite sure!" the deep, velvety voice replied.

When she had been introduced Una had proffered her hand, but then realised she had made a mistake and quickly withdrew it.

The carriage moved off and now in the light of the gas-lamps shining in through the windows, she had a quick glimpse of the woman sitting next to her.

She was enveloped in scarlet ostrich feathers and her face was very thin with a straight, thin nose in the centre of it.

But her eyes, dark and slanting upwards with eyelashes that were heavily mascaraed, made Una think that she was different from anyone she had ever seen or imagined in her whole life.

On her dark hair she wore a hat over which more crimson feathers cascaded and it was set at an angle that was both provocative and daring.

In the light of every lamp they passed, Una could see a little more, and now she was conscious of a heavy perfume which seemed to pervade the whole carriage with an exotic fragrance that was cloying and inescapable.

Philippe Dubucheron watched the women with a smile on his face and they drove in silence for only a short distance before they turned in through a gateway.

There was a courtyard, then the entrance to the house blazing with light, with a red carpet beside which six footmen with powdered wigs and white satin breeches were waiting to help them alight.

"At least your Duke has style," the woman with the ostrich feathers remarked.

Then she alighted, her crimson feathers floating about her like little tongues of fire.

It was quite obvious, Una thought, that she considered her not worth speaking to.

Because she was nervous, not only of the strange woman, but also of the grandeur of the house, she moved a little slowly as she stepped from the carriage.

Philippe Dubucheron sensed what she was feeling and said:

"It is all right! Do not be nervous. I should have warned you that Yvette Joyant does not like other women."

"Perhaps she would rather . . . I had not . . . come," Una said in a whisper.

"The Duke is your host," Monsieur Dubucheron replied, "and she is only another guest, just as you are."

They were walking as they spoke down a corridor decorated with magnificent pieces of furniture and huge vases of flowers whose fragrance Una thought was far preferable to the perfume used by Yvette Joyant.

Then she told herself she should not be critical. This was all new to her and therefore rather frightening, but at the same time, exciting.

She was to meet a Duke and an English one at that. That should please her mother and, even if she never saw him again or went to another house half as impressive as this, it would always be something to remember.

She heard the Clerk of the Chambers announcing the Duke's guests.

"Mademoiselle Yvette Joyant, Your Grace. Mademoiselle Una Thoreau, Monsieur Philippe Dubucheron!"

For a moment there was so much to look

at, that Una found it hard to focus her eyes. Then in a kaleidoscope of elegant furniture, flowers, pictures, china and mirrors she saw a man.

He was, she thought with a leap of her heart, exactly how an Englishman and a Duke should look.

He was tall, handsome, magnificent in his evening clothes, and somehow, in a way she could not explain even to herself, so overpowering that she felt inexpressibly shy.

Una was never shy as a rule. She found everyone she met interesting, and even the long tales of their childhood the Nuns would relate when they had the chance, could always hold her attention and her imagination.

Now as she reached the Duke and he turned his eyes from Yvette Joyant to her, she felt her self-confidence leave her and it was impossible to look him in the face as she had intended to do.

Her mother had said to her often enough:

"Always look at the people with whom you shake hands and remember that shyness is merely being selfish. You are thinking of yourself and not of the person to whom you are talking."

She had therefore, always shaken hands in the manner her mother had taught her and looked at the person to whom she was being introduced in the face and with a smile on her lips.

Now she took the Duke's hand, but it was impossible to look at him and her eye-lashes were dark against the paleness of her cheeks.

"I am delighted to meet you, Miss Thoreau!" the Duke was saying. "I am lucky enough to possess two of your father's pictures and I can only offer you my sincerest condolences on his death."

"Thank . . . you," Una said in a low voice.

Then because she was ashamed of her own stupidity, she forced herself to look up at the Duke and to meet his eyes.

He was looking at her with an expression she could not understand. It was almost as if he looked her over in the same way that Monsieur Dubucheron had done.

But there was also, she thought, a faintly mocking twist to his lips that she could not exactly call a smile.

The Duke shook hands with Philippe Dubucheron and then as the servants brought them glasses of champagne, Yvette Joyant was talking to the Duke in a soft, velvety undertone which showed only too clearly that what she said was for his ears, and his ears alone.

Una moved a little nearer to Philippe Dubucheron.

"Do you think," she said, "that Papa's picture will be hung here in this room?"

She looked round as she spoke, seeing that the pictures were nearly all in keeping with the style of the furniture.

"I doubt it," Philippe Dubucheron replied. "I think His Grace will take the pictures with him to England."

"Are you talking about your father's pictures?" the Duke asked.

"I was . . . wondering," Una replied, "whether you would hang the one Your Grace has just bought in this room."

"As a matter of fact, I thought it would be out of place and the wrong period for this Salon," the Duke explained. "You are interested in pictures? You are yourself an artist?"

"I would like to be able to paint," Una answered, "but I have not Papa's talent. He found my efforts, when I tried to copy his pictures, very, very amateurish."

The Duke smiled.

"It is always a mistake to try to emulate one's parents," he said. "My father tried to make me into a cricketer and as a result cricket is a game I detest, which you must admit is very un-English."

"But you patronise 'The Sport of Kings',"

Philippe Dubucheron said. "I have read of your successes in the newspapers. You expect to do well this year?"

"I would like to win the Gold Cup at Ascot," the Duke replied, "but at least fifty other owners wish the same thing."

"You are not talking to me," Yvette Joyant pouted, "and if you want my opinion, I find men far more attractive than horses."

"That I can well believe," the Duke said.

She put up her hand covered in a long black glove and touched his shoulder.

"You like sports, Monsieur?" she asked. "I can show you some which are very original, *très amusants,* but only for the connoisseur."

She gave Una a disparaging glance as if she resented the fact that the Duke had been talking to her.

"*La jeune fille* is listening to what I have to say to you, Monsieur," she said, "and little pitchers have long ears!"

It was the French version of the old English adage, and was offensive in a way which made the blood come into Una's cheeks. She turned aside.

Monsieur Dubucheron had been right when he said that Mademoiselle Yvette did not like women.

At the same time, Una thought, it would be uncomfortable if she was going to jibe and jeer at her throughout the whole evening.

She suddenly felt that in a way she wished she had not come, then she told herself she was being absurd.

What could be more exciting and more interesting than to meet an English Duke, to see his magnificent French house, and to be, for the first time in her life, at a really grown-up dinner party?

"Why should I care what this Frenchwoman says to me?" she asked herself. "After all, I shall probably never see her again after tonight."

Her chin went up with an unconscious pride which would not permit her to be brow-beaten. She smiled at Philippe Dubucheron and said quietly:

"It is very exciting to be here, to see such lovely things all around us. Did you provide this house with all the pictures?"

"Unfortunately, no," Philippe Dubucheron replied. "I believe the Duke inherited most of them. The house was bought over fifty years ago by his grandfather."

"I am sure it has a history before that," Una said. "Mama told me about another house in this street which belonged to the

Princess Pauline Borghese and which was bought by the Duke of Wellington for the British Embassy."

"That is true," the Duke said, who apparently had been listening to the conversation. "The Embassy is two doors away, but I like to think that my house is larger and more attractive."

"Has it a very interesting history?" Una asked.

The Duke was about to answer when Yvette Joyant interrupted again.

"I will tell you a history that will make you laugh," she said. "The history of a man and of a woman who might easily, if we twist the facts a little, be you and me!"

There was something very caressing and very personal in her voice and the slant of her eyes, but before the Duke could reply, dinner was announced.

3

At dinner Yvette Joyant monopolized the conversation and made it very clear both to Una and to Philippe Dubucheron that they were too unimportant to be of any consequence.

The Duke listened to what she had to say with a cynical smile on his face which made Una feel that he was in some ways rather frightening.

She had never met anybody before who managed to seem aloof even when he was taking part in the conversation.

He appeared, she thought, to be watching everything that was taking place as if it was a theatrical performance and he was in the audience rather than being a participant.

She wondered if, in fact, that was how he always looked at life, or if it was just because this evening was unusual.

Perhaps a small party of four people was indeed unusual to the Duke who, she felt instinctively, was always the centre of a crowd of people listening to him and of course, admiring him.

The Dining-Room in the house was as magnificent as the Salon.

There were fine pictures on the walls, this time of a later period in French art, and the gold plate which decorated the table was the work of the great French craftsmen whom Una had read about.

She found it difficult not to stare around her in what her mother would have thought a vulgar manner.

But everything was so unusual and exciting that she had to force herself to appreciate the delicacies of the dishes that were, she knew, culinary masterpieces.

Her father had always enjoyed good cooking and had said over and over again in the past:

"One of the few consolations of living in France is that one can eat food that is not only a delight to the eyes, but a pleasure to the palate."

Her mother had laughed in response and replied:

"Personally, Julius, I would give up all these artistic creations for a slice of really good roast beef and some Yorkshire pudding."

She said it to tease her husband and he held up his hands in horror.

But because of hearing such conversations Una had learnt to cook the dishes her father liked from an old woman who came to their house more to oblige than because she needed the money.

It was her mother who had discovered that Madame Reynard had, at one time when her husband was alive, had a Restaurant in Paris.

She had retired to the village to spend her last years talking of the past and of all the important people who had patronised their Restaurant because the owner was an exceptionally good Chef.

She however, had found time heavy on her hands with nothing to do and although she was too grand to help with the cleaning of the house or even the kitchen, she would cook, as Una's father said, 'like an angel' and so Una became her pupil.

She thought as she sampled a dish of Loire salmon stuffed with oysters and truffles, that if only her father was alive, she would have been able to copy it for him.

As if the Duke sensed what she was thinking, he asked:

"Besides painting, I appreciate good food, Miss Thoreau."

She smiled at him as she replied:

"I admit to being greedy when the food is

as delicious as this!"

"You speak as if that is something new," the Duke remarked.

"I have been living in Italy, Your Grace, and Italian food, however hard it tries, can never be as good as the French."

"That is what I have found," the Duke agreed.

"But Italians make good lovers!" Yvette Joyant interposed. "And so do Englishmen when they take the trouble."

She spoke in a provocative manner in her deep velvety voice and her eyes looking at the Duke promised exotic delights. He understood all too well what she was saying to him.

He thought that Philippe Dubucheron had been right when he said the contrast between the two women would be remarkable.

It would have been impossible, the Duke thought, to find such a contrast by chance and he supposed that Philippe Dubucheron had planned what was happening very carefully.

He had known with his shrewd understanding that no man could fail to be intrigued if he was confronted with Yvette and Una at the same time.

The Duke did not believe for one moment that Una had arrived in Paris unexpectedly as Philippe Dubucheron had said.

He had doubtless known of her for a long time and had been keeping her in the background for just such an occasion as this.

If he himself had not come to Paris at this precise moment, then probably this dinner-party would have been taking place with another rich and distinguished man at the head of the table.

He did not trust Dubucheron, the Duke thought. At the same time there was no doubt that the evening, though different from what he had planned, would prove amusing.

At least tomorrow he would be in a position to tell Beaumont that he had been to the cross-roads and which way he had turned.

Yvette Joyant, he thought, was original among the *demi-mondaines* with whom Paris abounded.

The Duke, like most Englishmen, came to Paris to amuse himself and amusement invariably meant meeting the Courtesans who were the Queens of their profession.

Each woman was an expert in *les sciences galantes,* considered her beauty her capital and made it pay breathtaking dividends.

He was quite certain that Yvette would extract every penny that was possible from him, but undoubtedly for most men the experience would be worth while.

If Philippe Dubucheron had said she was exceptional in that she was the most evil woman in Paris, then indeed she would be.

The Duke appreciated that she was indeed expert at creating an atmosphere round her that would make the man she wished to attract at least curious.

Every word she spoke had a *double entendre,* every look she gave him was calculated to arouse his senses and make the blood run a little faster in his veins.

The words she whispered continually in his ear were inflammatory in a manner that the Duke knew would have had, if he had not been so experienced where women were concerned, the result she intended.

He had in fact, known so many women in the same category as Yvette, and as he found women on the whole were much the same whether they were in Buckingham Palace or the Moulin Rouge, he was not swept off his feet by everything Yvette Joyant offered to him.

At the same time *l'amour,* concerning which the French considered they knew more than anyone else, could be always new, always exciting even when it was unlikely that anything as far as the Duke was concerned would be a surprise.

Una, on the other hand he thought, would only surprise him if she was really as innocent and as young as she looked.

He was quite sure that Philippe Dubucheron had dressed her for the part she had to play.

The Duke had not missed the fact that Una's gown was that of a very young girl, modest and yet undoubtedly becoming.

His eyes noted the tiny waist, the way in which the tight bodice revealed her small breasts.

The décolletage was that of a *jeune fille* who had no idea that her mission in life was to attract men, while her hair, although extremely becoming, was obviously her own effort and not that of a hairdresser.

At the same time he was not entirely sure.

Philippe Dubucheron was a very astute man and would be likely, the Duke thought, to have anticipated that his client satiated with the familiar degradations of Paris, might be amused by purity and innocence.

'But is Una in fact, either pure or innocent?' he asked himself.

Judging by her gown and her behaviour she might be a well-rehearsed theatrical edition of what youth and innocence should look like.

Dubucheron had deceived him once and the Duke told himself he had no intention of being taken for 'a mug' a second time.

Yet it was impossible to believe, unless this girl was a young Rachel or Sarah Bernhardt, that she could act so convincingly.

Just as Yvette exuded an atmosphere of eroticism, Una appeared to be enveloped by an aura of purity.

Because he was interested in both women, the Duke began to enjoy himself and to forget his boredom and his anger with Rose Caversham.

Also the slight fatigue he had felt after his long journey was beginning to disappear with what he ate and drank.

Besides the delectable enticements on either side of him, he also enjoyed talking to Philippe Dubucheron.

He had used the man for some years as a purveyor of pictures, information about Paris, and frankly as a procurer of women.

But he was astute enough to realise that Dubucheron was in fact, an interesting character, the type of man who had been created by Paris itself.

He could not really be found in any other Capital in the world, and it was because he was unique that the Duke wished to probe into his brain and find out exactly why he was as he was.

By the end of dinner he began vaguely to understand that to Philippe Dubucheron life was a huge and amusing joke and the laughter he created paid him very large dividends.

He was not just a seeker after wealth but, the Duke thought, a man who saw life in all its aspects, as a pageant passing before him which enriched not only his pocket but also his mind.

Philippe Dubucheron was therefore a very different person from the men who usually availed themselves of his hospitality to talk of sport because they knew it interested him and of women because there they stood on common ground.

The Duke had long prided himself on being a judge of character.

But perhaps because he had probed deeply into the characters of some of his so-called friends and some of the women who had said they loved him, it had made him more cynical than he had been before.

It was amazing, he thought, how petty and how avaricious even the nicest people could be.

He often accused himself of being ultra-critical and though he would not have admitted it to Mr Beaumont, of expecting far more from those he knew than they were capable of giving.

He understood only too well exactly what his Comptroller had been saying to him today.

Yet he asked himself whether any life he chose to live would not after a time be just as monotonous and with 'a sameness' that was inevitable.

But here tonight, he thought towards the end of the dinner, were two women who were a little different.

He began to wonder as Yvette talked to him, whether there were erotic depths to which he had not yet descended but were there for him to discover.

He also found that Una's performance was even more incredible, unless of course, he was mistaken and she really was what she appeared to be.

Then he told himself the excellent wines they were drinking must have gone to his head, or else the trap that Philippe Dubucheron had set for him was even more cleverly baited than he anticipated.

As the dinner ended he knew from the way Dubucheron looked at him that he was expected to make a decision as to whether he would continue the evening with one of the women or the other.

It therefore amused the Duke to say as they drank their coffee:

"I think as it is my first night in Paris, for some time, I should visit the old familiar haunts and see if they have changed since I last patronised them."

"Which haunts in particular?" Philippe Dubucheron enquired.

The Duke smiled at him mockingly.

"Surely that is an unnecessary question. Where else but the Moulin Rouge?"

Yvette made an expression of disgust.

"The Moulin Rouge!" she said. "I will take you somewhere where we can see an exhibition that will be different from anything you have ever seen before."

Her mascaraed eyes slanted mysteriously as she said:

"We will go alone, then you will see."

The Duke allowed her to think for one moment that he would accept her invitation. Then he said:

"You cannot expect me to abandon my friends. No, we will go together, all four of us to the Moulin Rouge."

Yvette shrugged her shoulders, but there was undoubtedly a glint of anger in her eyes and her lips tightened ominously.

She had been so sure when Dubucheron had told her she was to dine with the Duke of Wolstanton that by the end of the evening, she would be his mistress and the large pile of debts that was accumulating in her apartment would have a likelihood of being paid.

Her extravagance was the talk of Paris, but that in one way was her attraction.

Every *demi-mondaine* knew that men only appreciated what they had to pay for 'through the nose'!

The diamonds around Yvette's neck and those that encircled her wrists had all been part of a payment which entitled a man to boast amongst his friends that 'Yvette Joyant had cost him a packet'.

It had been established in the Second Empire that the Courtesans of Paris were the most expensive and the most sensual in the world.

Then Napoleon III had set the pace by spending a fortune on his many mistresses, to be followed by the Prince Napoleon and every other man who visited Paris in search of amusement.

The golden era was followed by a depression which was only now getting back into its stride, but Yvette knew that being the head of her profession, she was in fact worth all the millions of francs which were spent on her.

To be under the protection of the Duke of Wolstanton would, she knew, give her a new prestige, quite apart from that if Philippe Dubucheron had said he was rich, then he was very rich indeed.

She did not, for a moment, suspect that the Duke might not be interested in her.

She only thought it a bore that they must be accompanied by a tiresome young girl, while Dubucheron should stay in his proper place and not intrude where he was not wanted.

Una's eyes however, lit up with excitement.

She had always longed to go to the Moulin Rouge, even though she knew the idea of it would have shocked her mother.

She had however, thought that if she came to live with her father in Montmartre he might take her to the place that typified the Paris which until now, had been nothing in her life except a name.

She did not realise while she was looking at the Duke, that Philippe Dubucheron was looking at her.

He did not quite understand what game the Duke was playing, but he was well aware the Moulin Rouge was not the right place for Una.

He was, in fact, a little nervous of her reaction.

He knew as the Duke did, that the Moulin Rouge had become of interest to upper-class gentlemen simply because it was the biggest market of prostitution in Europe.

The girls there were almost as expensive as those in the Champs Élysées, but the Cabaret was good and the artists like Toulouse Lautrec who drew the posters for it, were making it more fashionable year by year.

Toulouse Lautrec's poster had not exaggerated when it promised that the Moulin was, *'Le Rendezvous de Highlife'*.

But if the Duke wished to go to the Moulin Rouge, Philippe Dubucheron had no intention of trying to prevent him.

The evening had been a surprise from the very beginning and he told himself that he was not prepared to argue with the Duke, whatever he might suggest.

Although he thought it was slightly out of character for a man who he sensed was extremely fastidious, it was after all to be expected of every Englishman, that he should, when he arrived in Paris, gravitate towards the Moulin Rouge as a mouse towards cheese.

The Duke's carriage was waiting, and it was far larger and more comfortable than Philippe Dubucheron's.

At the same time, the latter had expected that the Duke would suggest that they should go in two carriages and his own was waiting in the courtyard.

Without his asking the question, the Duke gave him the answer.

"We will travel together. There is room on my back seat for three if they are not too fat."

He glanced as he spoke, at Yvette's sinuous figure and at Una's childish one. Then he seated himself between the two ladies while Philippe Dubucheron sat opposite to them.

During the drive from the Rue du Faubourg St Honoré to Montmartre, Yvette took the opportunity of whispering in the Duke's ear words which it was fortunate Una could not overhear.

As a matter of fact it was unlikely that she would have understood much of what was said.

She was actually looking out of the windows, entranced once again by the brilliantly lit Boulevards, by the processions of people parading up and down the broad pavements, by the crowded Cafés, and by everything which spoke to her of Paris.

It was, she thought, the most exciting evening she had ever spent and for the moment she was prepared to forget the morrow and all the difficulties that lay ahead and enjoy each moment as it passed.

While Yvette was as close to the Duke as possible, seeming to entwine herself round him, Una sat in a corner of the carriage so that her body did not touch his.

At the same time, she was vividly conscious that she was beside him and that in a way she could not understand he made her feel a little strange.

She kept telling herself it was because he was English and with the exception of her father, different from any other man she had seen before.

He did in fact, remind her of what her father had been like when she was small, when she had loved the sound of his voice and the way he picked her up in his arms.

She could not have been very old when she first realised her father looked different, very different from the Frenchmen she saw when she walked in the village, or even when very occasionally she went with her mother into the City of Paris.

Julius Thoreau, besides being broad-shouldered and good-looking, had always had a presence about him.

"I fell in love with your father," her mother said once, "because he was so handsome, and then I love him because he is the kindest as well as the most attractive man in the world."

Looking back it seemed to Una that even before her mother's death her father had begun to change.

It was not only the strange clothes he affected because he was an artist. He seemed to lose some of his English characteristics.

And yet, she told herself now, it was wrong of her to criticise him.

The Duke was everything she had always thought an English gentleman was like, in addition to being a Duke, and she thought too there was something straight-forward and honest about him.

This was different from what she felt about Monsieur Dubucheron even though he had been so kind.

She wondered if the Duke liked Mademoiselle Joyant touching him with her black-gloved hands, and if he felt embarrassed by the very proprietary way in which she was behaving.

She felt her mother would have thought it rather ill-bred, but again she told herself she had no right to find fault.

It was so kind, so very kind of the Duke to have asked her to dinner.

She wanted to talk to him about pictures,

especially her father's, but it would have been difficult to talk of anything serious when Mademoiselle Joyant was listening.

'I wonder if I shall ever see him again after this evening is over?' Una thought wistfully.

Then they arrived at the Moulin Rouge.

It was very much bigger than she had expected, as large as the Railway Station at which she had arrived in Paris, and the noise as they entered was almost deafening.

Philippe Dubucheron arranged that they were escorted through the crowds and given what was considered one of the best tables at the side of the dance-floor.

Una recognised the Band was playing one of Offenbach's romantic tunes.

It sounded very different from the way she had heard it before, yet it managed to be heard amongst the chatter of voices and the raucous laughter which seemed to rise in a crescendo over everything else.

They had only just sat down when there was a roll of the drums and La Goulue, one of the new stars at the Moulin, appeared on the dance-floor.

"She is only twenty years old," Una heard Philippe Dubucheron tell the Duke.

Then she found herself gasping at the manner in which the girl danced.

Plump white skirts six yards wide, of

swirling lace springing out of a tumbled froth of black expensive undergarments trimmed with delicately coloured ribbons moved as she swung up her leg pointing it straight at the chandelier.

It was a well-shaped leg held stiff and straight, gleaming silkily and caught above the knee by a garter of diamonds.

Voluptuous, gay, tumultuous, provocative, it was the sort of dance that Una had never imagined could even exist.

She did not realise that it was in fact extremely improper. It only seemed to leave her breathless and while the crowds shouted: "Higher, La Goulue. Higher!" she was too bemused even to clap her hands.

La Goulue kicked her leg, displayed her drawers with a jerk of the hips and revealed a heart embroidered on her behind. It brought a roar from those watching that seemed to shake the very roof.

Next came the Can-Can which had become, as Philippe Dubucheron knew, a kind of ritual dance, made as erotic as possible and far more suggestive than it had been originally.

But it had a gaiety that was indescribable and an undoubted skill in a performance which ended in the splits.

Sitting very straight on the hard chair,

Una stared at what was taking place in front of her, her hands clasped together in her lap, a glass of champagne untouched in front of her.

She did not realise that the Duke was watching her even while Yvette whispered in his ear, or that Philippe Dubucheron was watching her too.

She could only feel that this was the most fantastic and strange dancing she had ever seen in a very extraordinary place.

At the same time, she could understand that artists like her father would find a hundred different faces and poses there which would make a picture.

When the Cabaret came to an end and the crowd moved onto the dance-floor, she said to Monsieur Dubucheron:

"Will you point out to me any painters who are here tonight?"

He looked around.

"Toulouse Lautrec will be somewhere. He is always here two or three times a week, and if I can see him, I will show you also Degas, who was a friend of your father's, and the caricaturist Metivet."

"Thank you," Una said.

"Tell me what you think of the Moulin Rouge, if this is your first visit here?" the Duke asked.

There was a query in his words which Philippe Dubucheron did not miss.

Una answered him quite honestly.

"It is difficult to put into words, Your Grace, what it makes me feel," she said, "but I can understand how artists could find it interesting."

"Why?"

"The people . . . the performers, they have such individual faces," she answered. "They are not like the people one sees elsewhere."

She thought the Duke looked sceptical, and she added quickly:

"At least, not the sort of people I have met . . . but then that is not surprising."

"You have come from Italy," he said, "but where in Italy?"

She was unable to answer him before Yvette demanded his attention and again he was listening to something she was whispering to him.

While he was doing so, a gentleman resplendent in evening clothes, a top-hat at an angle on his head, came up to the table.

"Hello, Blaze," he said to the Duke. "I did not expect to see you here. I thought you were in London."

"And so I was until yesterday."

His friend however, was not listening to

his reply. He had taken Yvette Joyant's hand in his and raised it to his lips.

"I am in luck in finding you here," he said, "became I intended to call on you tomorrow."

"I hope you will do that," Yvette replied.

"Come and dance with me," the newcomer said. "I have something important to tell you."

Yvette looked at the Duke from under her heavy eyelashes.

"Do you mind, *mon Cher?*" she asked, "or would you rather dance with me yourself?"

"I will watch you," the Duke replied.

She hesitated as if she debated whether she would demand that he dance with her.

Then obviously determined to make him realise what he was missing, she held out her arms to the man who was standing by the table.

"Let us show them, Henri, how two bodies can move as one," she said.

She moved into his arms, then had a provocative look at the Duke from over her shoulder, as they moved away amongst the dancers.

The Duke looked across the table at Philippe Dubucheron.

"I think, Dubucheron," he said, "that Miss Thoreau should have an early night.

Shall I take her home?"

There was a touch of laughter in Philippe Dubucheron's eyes as he replied:

"It would be very gracious of Your Grace but unfortunately at the moment, she has no home."

"What do you mean?" the Duke enquired.

"She arrived today as I have already told you," Dubucheron answered, "and I was intending, when the evening ended, to find her a respectable lodging. Her trunk, as it happens, is at your house. I thought I would collect it later."

There was a smile on the Duke's lips which echoed the expression in his eyes.

"My house?" he said with raised eyebrows, "and would you consider that a respectable place for Miss Thoreau to spend the night?"

"It would certainly be more comfortable than anywhere I could suggest."

"I cannot quite make up my mind," the Duke said, "whether you are extremely astute, clairvoyant, or merely damned impertinent."

Philippe Dubucheron's gesture was too French to need the accompaniment of words.

"Very well," the Duke said, rising to his

feet. "Give my apologies to Mademoiselle Yvette and assure her that I will express my gratitude for the pleasure of her company in an appropriate manner."

"She will be disappointed," Philippe Dubucheron answered, "but doubtless any hard feelings can be placated in the usual manner."

"Of course," the Duke replied. "And I am sure tomorrow you will call with the pictures you promised to let me see."

"I shall be with Your Grace," Philippe Dubucheron replied.

The Duke turned to look at Una and found to his surprise that she was not listening to the conversation that was taking place, but staring across the dance-floor.

"I am sure," she exclaimed excitedly, "that that must be Monsieur Toulouse-Lautrec. He looks just as Papa described him to me, and he is sketching someone who is dancing."

Philippe Dubucheron followed the direction of her eyes.

"Yes, that is Lautrec," he answered. "It is not surprising that his family are appalled by his appearance."

The dwarf wearing his bowler hat, with his two tiny legs and disproportionately large head, his thick nose on which rested steel-rimmed pince-nez and his bushy black beard, looked grotesque.

"He cannot help his appearance," Una said compassionately.

She would have said more, but she realised the Duke was standing on his feet and looked up at him.

"I am taking you home," he said quietly.

"Thank you," she replied.

Only as she started to move away from the table did she realise that Philippe Dubucheron was not following them.

She looked back in consternation.

"It is all right," he said quickly. "The Duke will look after you and your trunk is at his house."

"Where am I . . . staying?"

"The Duke will tell you," Dubucheron replied. "Follow His Grace. He does not like to be kept waiting."

"No, of course not."

Una picked up her shawl which she had laid on the back of her chair and hurried after the Duke who was already wending his way between the tables towards the exit.

It was impossible to speak as they pushed through the crowds of men; most were in evening clothes wearing top-hats, but among them there were some strange types with floppy ties and velvet suits.

Champagne corks popped, the multi-coloured crowd was reflected along one wall which was entirely covered with mirrors.

There was a short pause at the door while the Duke's carriage was brought to them, then they were driving away and there was more room on the back seat than there had been when it had held three.

"Thank you very much for such an interesting, exciting evening!" Una said in a soft little voice.

"You enjoyed it?" the Duke asked.

"I enjoyed dining at your house more than anything I have ever done," she replied. "But the Moulin Rouge is something I had always longed to see."

"Why?"

"Because Papa told me about it, and even the girls at School had heard of it."

"School?" the Duke asked.

"I have been at School in Florence for the last three years," Una explained.

The Duke was silent for a moment. Then he said:

"Did Philippe Dubucheron tell you to tell me that?"

Una looked puzzled.

"No, why should he? But I thought he might have told Your Grace that I came to Paris . . . because Papa sent for me . . . only to find he was . . . dead."

There was a little throb in her voice which the Duke did not miss.

"Tell me what happened from the beginning."

"When Mama died . . ." Una began.

She told him simply and in a few words how her mother had left all her money to pay for her education and she had been sent to the Convent in Florence.

Only when her father had sent her a telegram in answer to her letter telling him she was too old to stay there any longer, had she come back to France.

She did not realise that because she told the story so simply and in so few words, the Duke was immediately suspicious.

It was all too pat, too glib, he thought.

An innocent young girl arrives in Paris to find her father dead and Dubucheron, a notorious procurer, takes her that very night to dine with a Duke.

If Una found it surprising he found it incredible, and he lay back in the carriage watching her profile silhouetted against the gas-lights as they passed them.

It had been clever, he thought, of Dubucheron to tell her not to wear a hat when every other woman in Paris had an evening hat that varied from every sort of exotic feather to clusters of artificial flowers.

Once again the Duke thought he was being trapped by Dubucheron, but at least, he told himself, the bait was original and not a variation of the same old theme as Yvette Joyant had been.

He had decided suddenly, although he was not quite certain why, that Yvette not only failed to excite him, but that he actually found her repulsive.

The things she had said to him were lewd and licentious beyond anything he had ever heard in a very varied career.

He had known that they should have amused him because her deep velvety voice took the edge off them, but all the time, she was talking he had been acutely conscious of the young girl sitting on his other side.

Una had not made the slightest effort to attract his attention or assert her personality.

That perhaps was the reason why he found it hard to take his eyes off her.

But it was just too good a story, he told himself, as she finished speaking. However it would be a pity, to show her too quickly that he was not deceived.

If that was the game she wanted to play — he would go along with it. Aloud he said:

"It must have been a great shock to you to

learn when you arrived in Paris that your father was dead."

"I find it difficult to believe," Una replied, "but I had not seen him for three years and I think he . . . must have . . . changed."

"Why should you think that?"

"His Studio was not the sort of place he would have . . . tolerated when Mama was alive."

"So the sight of his Studio prevented you from being unhappy?"

"I was unhappy," Una said, "but somehow I felt as if I had lost Papa a long time ago."

Her voice held just the right note of regret and her explanation was logical and, the Duke thought, understandable.

Again he told himself it was all too glib, with too many coincidences.

It was a coincidence that she should have arrived in Paris on the same day he had; that just the sort of picture he liked to buy was available; and that he himself had no particular plans for the evening.

Of course Dubucheron had this girl up his sleeve waiting for some mug to come along and find her different from the ordinary prostitute.

Besides what girl coming straight from a

Convent would go off alone with him in a carriage with nowhere to stay except, as Dubucheron intended, with him?

It would have been inconceivable for the Duke to take a woman who was his mistress to any of his other houses, but Paris was different.

He had always made it quite clear both to his Comptroller and to his friends that in Paris he reserved the right to act as he pleased with no questions asked.

When a little over a year ago he had been amused by a very delectable and charming dancer from the Théâtre des Variétés, she had stayed with him for a month.

Then when he returned to England she had moved back to her own apartment.

Dubucheron was obviously aware of this, yet the Duke thought that he had contrived that Una should move in with him in a manner that was a little clumsy.

The trunk left at his house, the information that he had made no arrangements for her before she came to dinner, her manner in being ready to go with him without explanation was all too contrived and he wondered what Dubucheron would have done if his choice had fallen on Yvette.

Then he told himself that had obviously been provided for as well.

"I am honoured," he said aloud, "that you should be willing to stay with me. You might have insisted that we get to know each other a little better first."

Una had been looking out of the window. Now she turned her face to his, but it was too dark for him to see the expression in her eyes.

"Stay with . . . you?" she queried. "Am I to stay with Your Grace . . . at your . . . house?"

"If that is what you would like to do."

"But of course . . . it would be wonderful!" she answered. "I never dreamt . . . I never thought . . . that you would . . . invite me to be your guest."

This, the Duke thought, was really straining credulity too far.

"I think that is perhaps what Dubucheron intended," he said, "and you must have been aware of it."

"He was very kind to me . . . when he found me in the Studio," Una answered, "and he told me when he sold Papa's picture that he would come back and make . . . plans for my . . . future."

The Duke did not speak and she added:

"You see . . . I had arrived in Paris with . . . very little money . . . and it was so very fortunate that Monsieur Dubucheron could sell Papa's picture."

"Very fortunate indeed," the Duke said, "and Dubucheron told you he would give you the money tomorrow?"

"Yes, that is what he said," Una answered, "so I should have been able to pay for . . . anywhere I stayed the night."

"And before you came to my house where did you change into your evening-gown?"

"Monsieur Dubucheron took me to his Art Gallery."

She gave a little laugh.

"It seemed a strange place to change one's clothes when it was all shut up, but I could wash there and unpack my trunk in his office."

The Duke did not believe a word of it.

He was quite certain that the whole story was a fabrication from start to finish.

He gave Dubucheron and Una full marks for working out a tale that sounded like an adventure story in some school-girl's journal.

Who had ever heard of someone changing their clothes in a Picture Gallery?

And who indeed, except Dubucheron, would have thought of anything so extraordinary as bringing a woman's trunk to the place where she had dinner?

He wanted to laugh aloud, but he told

himself that to expose Una's ingenious little tale too soon would spoil the fun.

They arrived at his house in the Rue du Faubourg St Honoré, and as they entered the Hall the Duke said to the waiting servants:

"I understand that a trunk was left here before dinner?"

"Yes, Your Grace," the Clerk of the Chambers replied. "The gentleman said he might call for it later tonight."

"I have arranged for Mademoiselle Thoreau to stay here," the Duke said. "Have her trunk taken to the *Chambre des Roses* and unpacked."

"Very good, Your Grace."

"Let us go into the Salon," the Duke said to Una and he walked ahead to open the door before an attentive footman could reach it.

The Salon was fragrant with flowers, and only a few lights were left burning.

It looked so lovely that Una stood looking around her with an expression of admiration on her face, her eyes shining.

The Duke went to a corner of the room where on a tray was an opened bottle of champagne in an ice-bucket and a silver dish containing pâté sandwiches.

"Are you hungry?" he asked.

"No, thank you," Una replied. "It was such a delicious dinner, and I would like to thank your Chef for cooking something so delectable."

"You can thank him tomorrow," the Duke said. "I am sure he will be delighted."

He walked back towards her as he spoke and handed her a glass of champagne.

"Please . . . I would rather not have any . . . more," she said. "I am not used to drinking anything but . . . water."

The corners of the Duke's mouth twisted.

"Champagne is the water of France."

"So I have always been told," Una replied, "but I am afraid it might go to my head."

"Has that happened before?"

She gave a little laugh.

"Never, as it happens, but then I have never had more than an occasional sip of champagne to drink! I should feel very ashamed if I felt muzzy or stupid."

"Ashamed?" the Duke enquired.

"I think drink can be horrible and degrading," she said in a different tone of voice.

She had a sudden vision as she spoke of the empty bottles in her father's Studio and the terrible blotched picture standing on the easel.

The Duke guessed what she was thinking, remembering that Dubucheron had said that her father had died when he was dead drunk.

He sat himself in a chair and asked:

"Now you are staying with me what do you intend to do about it?"

As he asked the question, he knew quite well how it would have been answered by Yvette, and it amused him to speculate how long this girl would keep up her presence of being so innocent.

Una looked at him with an expression of perplexity in her eyes.

Then as he did not suggest it, she sat down a little nervously on the edge of a chair.

For a moment she did not speak, then suddenly her expression altered.

"Now I . . . understand," she said. "You must have thought me very . . . stupid."

"In what way?" the Duke asked.

"I told Monsieur Dubucheron that I must find a job of some sort, so as to earn money, and yet it never struck me that I could find one with you."

"What are you suggesting you should do for me?" the Duke asked.

"I . . . I am not quite . . . certain," she replied. "When I was sitting in the Studio while Monsieur Dubucheron was selling Papa's picture I thought that the only possible thing I could do would be to teach children to speak English. But then. . . ."

She stopped, and the Duke prompted:

"Then what did you think?"

"I was afraid perhaps I looked . . . too young."

"And what do you imagine you could do for me?"

"I could write your letters. I really write very well."

"I have an excellent Comptroller who does them," the Duke replied, "and if necessary he has a secretary who I believe has been employed for some years when we are in Paris."

Una thought for a moment, then she gave a little sigh.

"There are so . . . many things I cannot do well," she said, "but anyway, I do not expect you would want them."

"Such as?" the Duke asked.

"I can play the piano a little. I can paint, but it is very amateurish, and Papa said I would never make an artist."

"I could hardly expect you to paint pictures for me," the Duke said, "and I am sure Dubucheron can supply me with any painting that takes my fancy."

"No, of course not!" Una agreed. "I was only trying to tell you what I cannot do."

"Then suppose we skip that and get to what you can?"

She gave him an agonised little look.

"The truth . . . is," she said in a forlorn voice, "that although Mama spent so much money on my education I cannot . . . think how to use . . . any of it!"

"Have you ever looked in the mirror?" the Duke asked.

She stared at him in surprise, then she answered:

"But of course! When I do my hair."

"Look into it now," he said, "and tell me what you see."

Una got to her feet.

Then because she was not very tall she stood on tip-toe to look between the Sèvres clock and the other ornaments on the shelf at the huge gilt-framed mirror that hung above on the marble mantelpiece.

She stared at her reflection and thought, as she did so, that she had never seen herself with such an alluring background.

With its painted ceiling, the pictures on the walls, the heavy French silk curtains, it was just the sort of room she had always longed to live in and which her mother would have loved too.

"Well?" the Duke asked from behind her.

She turned to flash him a smile.

"I am sorry," she said. "I was not looking at myself. I was looking at your wonderful room. It is just like one of Boucher's pictures and I feel that I look almost like Madame du Pompadour. You remember the one he painted of her?"

"Perhaps that is something you could be," the Duke suggested.

"But the King loved her and there is no King in France today," Una replied. "And if I were Madame du Pompadour, I feel I would never be clever enough to suggest that the Sèvres china should be made pink like these lovely vases on your mantel-piece."

She put out her fingers to touch them very gently.

Watching her, the Duke thought she had a grace of movement that must have been taught in a Dramatic Academy. It was impossible for it to be natural.

Una gave a sigh that was a sound of delight. Then she said:

"I have a feeling I am keeping you up when you told Monsieur Dubucheron that you were tired. I am tired too, but everything here is so lovely that I want to touch your treasures, to look at them, and to tell myself stories of why they were made!"

"Even so, you would like to go to bed?" the Duke asked.

"They will all be here . . . tomorrow," Una replied, in a rapt little voice.

Then, as if she suddenly remembered what they had been talking about, she added:

"Thank you very much for having me here and by tomorrow, when I am not so sleepy, perhaps I can think of how I can work for you."

The Duke rose slowly to his feet and seemed about to speak. But before he could do so, Una clasped her hands together.

"I do hope Mama knows I am here," she said. "She would be so thrilled that I am staying with an Englishman like those she knew when she was a girl, and I think she would be . . . happy because although Papa is dead, I am safe . . . with you."

She looked up at him and there was a little pause while the Duke looked into her eyes in a searching manner which once again, made Una feel shy.

Then he said in a voice that had a note of surprise in it:

"Go to bed. We are both tired. We will talk about this tomorrow."

4

Una was awakened by a maid coming into her bedroom carrying her breakfast on a tray.

She put it down beside the bed and went to pull back the curtains so that the sunshine flooded in.

For a moment it was difficult for Una, still drowsy with sleep, to think where she was. Then with a leap of her heart she remembered.

She was in Paris and she was staying with the Duke of Wolstanton!

She sat up looking with delight at the neatly laid breakfast tray with its silver coffee-pot and hot croissants.

"What is the time?" she asked.

"*Dix heures*, M'mselle," the maid replied.

"Ten o'clock?" Una exclaimed in consternation. "How can it be? How can I have slept so late?"

"M'mselle was tired," the maid replied. "It is a lovely day and very warm."

"Ten o'clock!" Una repeated, then added tentatively, "Perhaps . . . Monsieur Le Duc will think it . . . rude that I have not gone down to breakfast."

The maid smiled.

"Monsieur has gone riding, M'mselle, so there is no hurry."

Una felt a sense of relief.

She realised that last night she should have asked the Duke what time she should have breakfast and if she had it with him.

She could not remember ever before having breakfast in bed, unless she was ill. When she lived at home with her father and mother they had always breakfasted together at eight o'clock.

She realised now that she had in fact felt very tired the previous evening.

It was not only the long journey when it had been difficult to sleep in the train, but also the emotions of the day had all taken their toll.

First the shock of her father's death, the realisation that she was suddenly alone and had nowhere to go.

Then there had been the excitement of dining with the Duke and going to the Moulin Rouge which she thought in retrospect was even more fantastic and more disreputable than she had expected it to be.

It was only when she was undressed and in bed that she had thought it had perhaps been very reprehensible of her to have visited a place of entertainment so soon after hers father's death.

Then she asked herself, in a practical manner, what else she could have done.

She knew instinctively that Monsieur Dubucheron and also the Duke would have thought it very tiresome if she had sat miserably mourning her father and had insisted on staying at home alone.

Then she remembered that she had no home, and if she had not done what Monsieur Dubucheron suggested, she had a feeling that he would not even have offered her the hospitality of his Art Gallery.

She was perceptive enough to realise that beneath his jovial and, when the Duke was there, ingratiating manner, Monsieur Dubucheron was ruthless and determined to get his own way.

She thought he would not hesitate to keep the sale of her father's pictures for his own advantage, if she did not do what he wished.

She was almost shocked at having such suspicions about anyone, especially of accusing someone like Monsieur Dubucheron of being what was to all intents and purposes dishonest.

But Una was intelligent and she could not help asking herself what would have happened to the money gained by the sale of her father's pictures if she had not turned up at that precise moment in his Studio.

It seemed unlikely that Monsieur Dubucheron who, if he had ever known of her existence, had never seen her, would have put himself to a great deal of trouble to find her and hand over the money which was hers legally.

'I must do what he wishes,' she thought a little apprehensively and wondered how long the money, when she received it, would last.

Of course it all depended on how she spent it and she thought how very fortunate it was that the Duke had been kind enough to have her to stay.

She wondered whether many other men would have been so generous to a girl they had met for the first time, especially someone who shared so little of his interests.

'He is not only having me to stay, but I also think he is going to find me employment,' Una thought.

The whole room was golden with sunshine because it was such an exciting idea.

To live in a house like this, to be surrounded by pictures such as before she had only seen in Art Galleries, was like moving into Paradise.

She offered up an earnest little prayer that it would not end too quickly.

She ate her breakfast, and then because the maid had said it was hot, she washed and dressed herself in the thinnest gown she possessed.

It was a very simple muslin and actually she had made it herself.

The Nuns who were characteristically skilled with their needles, had taught her how to sew with tiny, almost invisible stitches which, to them, were traditional.

Una had copied a gown belonging to one of her friends whose family were exceedingly rich and took their daughter, even though she was not yet a débutante, to the most expensive Couturiers in Rome.

Compared to the other girls, she seemed like a bird of Paradise amongst a flock of sparrows, but she loved Una and was only too delighted for her to copy her clothes.

Una was already dressed when the maid came into the room.

"You should have rung the bell, M'mselle," she said. "I would have helped you."

"I did not think of it," Una answered. "I am so used to dressing myself."

"You look very pretty," the maid said, "and I am sure Monsieur Le Duc will think so too."

"I hope so," Una replied.

Then as she went downstairs, she wondered if he was back from his ride and thought if he was, he would be in the Salon.

The Salon, however, was empty and because she could stare as much as she liked at the things which interested her, she started to wander around looking at the pictures and touching the objets d'art almost reverently.

Riding in the Bois the Duke raised his hat to a number of friends and acquaintances but did not, as they expected, stop to speak to them.

He had not come to Paris to be social and he also wanted to think.

He, too, had slept well. He had awakened early with a feeling of well-being and also with the thought that the day would be quite an interesting one.

He wondered, as he dressed, whether Una was disappointed that he had not come to her room as she might have expected.

Her surprise at his appearance, ostensibly to bid her good-night, he thought mockingly, would have been in keeping with the rest of her performance.

As he ate his breakfast alone, he wondered if, in fact, she was genuine, then told himself he was not such a credulous fool as to be taken in by Dubucheron for a second time.

Mr Beaumont came into the room when he was finishing his coffee.

"I hear you have a guest, Your Grace."

"I imagined you might be surprised," the Duke replied.

"Is it anyone who has been here before?" Mr Beaumont asked tentatively.

He was aware that the Duke disliked being questioned about his private affairs. At the same time, if anything ever went wrong it was immediately laid like a burden on his shoulders, and he wished to be prepared.

"No, you have never met her before," the Duke said. "Nor, in fact, had I until last night."

With difficulty Mr Beaumont restrained himself from remarking: 'That was quick work!' but the Duke obviously had nothing more to say.

He went from the room and out through the Hall to where a horse was waiting for him in the courtyard.

He always rode when he was in Paris and because of the precipitate haste with which he had left England, he had not yet had time to have his own horses brought across the Channel.

Mr Beaumont, mistrusting livery stables, had therefore asked one of the Duke's friends if he could borrow a mount for the next two days.

The Comte de Clerc had been only too pleased to oblige and the Duke's eyes brightened at the sight of a magnificent black stallion who was being kept under control with difficulty by two grooms.

He swung himself into the saddle and rode off.

Mr Beaumont, watching him go, thought it would be difficult to find anyone who looked finer or more at home on a horse.

'He will certainly be in a good temper when he returns,' he thought to himself.

Then he wondered curiously who was the woman whom the Duke had brought home last night.

He imagined it would be an actress or a dancer of some repute.

The Duke was seldom interested in a lower class of woman and certainly would not have invited one to his house.

In fact, Mr Beaumont was astonished that the Duke should have a guest considering what he had said to him, only yesterday.

He went to his office and learnt from the

Clerk of the Chambers, that Mademoiselle had not yet been called and asked to be informed when she came down the stairs.

He then settled himself down to cope with the enormous amount of detail that was involved in getting the house into running order.

Over an hour later, he was informed that Mademoiselle was in the Salon and rising from his desk, walked across the Hall.

As he went, he wondered what type had captivated the Duke's interest this time, for he was well aware that Paris had changed a great deal in the last few years.

The expression *'fin de siècle'* had become widely used in France and was usually applied to artistic and literary tendencies, but it also applied to a great number of other things, such as pessimism and decadence.

Studying the situation of France from England, Mr Beaumont had learnt that the *fin de siècle* had established a style of female beauty that appeared in countless paintings and novels.

This ideal woman was a combination of the *femme fatale,* Oriental and Madonna.

She was incarnated by Sarah Bernhardt in many of her Plays and there was a great fashion for Salomes, Ophelias, Sapphos and Sphynxes.

Besides this, there had arisen, which was unusual in France, a definite eroticism and abnormality which would, if they had understood it, certainly have shocked the much more prudish English.

It made Mr Beaumont wonder which of the many facets of the *fin de siècle* had appealed to the Duke.

There was just a chance that it might be one of the Pre-Raphaelite lily-like ladies, pale, languorous and willowy, who were attracting attention in England.

To Mr Beaumont their soulful looks and affected postures seemed too theatrical and he had always believed the Duke had felt the same.

Yet, when he opened the door of the Salon, he was full of curiosity to see what woman had so quickly taken the place of the beautiful but fiery Lady Rose.

The sunshine was pouring through the open windows and for a moment, he thought the servants had been mistaken and there was nobody there.

Then he saw someone at the far end of the Salon, standing completely still and staring up at a picture by Fragonard.

He shut the door behind him and the sound made her turn and he found himself looking at what, for the moment, he thought was only a child.

Then as he crossed the room, he saw she was in fact older, but not very much, and dressed like a school-girl she might have been little more than sixteen.

He had expected the Duke's guest to be unusual, but certainly not as unusual as this.

The oval face with its huge eyes, the small nose and perfectly curved lips, reminded him of one of Boucher's models rather than the heavier, more mature goddesses depicted by Fragonard.

"How do you do!" he said in French. "May I introduce myself? I am the Comptroller for Monsieur Le Duc."

Una gave him a little curtsey and held out her hand.

"I am Una Thoreau," she said in English.

"You are the daughter of Julius Thoreau, the artist?"

"Yes, that is right."

"Then I am delighted to make your acquaintance, Miss Thoreau," Mr Beaumont said.

"Did you know my father?"

"No, but I have admired his pictures, especially the one the Duke has just bought."

"I had not seen it until yesterday," Una said.

She thought Mr Beaumont looked surprised and explained:

"I came to Paris yesterday to stay with my . . . father, but when I . . . arrived, I found he was . . . dead!"

"Dead?" Mr Beaumont exclaimed, wondering why the Duke had not informed him of the fact.

"It was . . . a great shock," Una said. "I was told it was . . . an accident."

"I am very sorry," Mr Beaumont murmured.

He thought she looked a little lost and could not understand why, even if her father was dead, the Duke had brought Thoreau's daughter here.

But he told himself quickly that it was no business of his and it would be a great mistake for the Duke to think he was prying on one of his guests.

"I hope you have everything you require, Miss Thoreau," he said aloud. "If not, if you will ring the bell and tell one of the servants to send for me, I am at your command."

"Thank you very much," Una answered, "but I am enjoying looking at this lovely room and its pictures."

"His Grace should be returning in about half-an-hour or so," Mr Beaumont said, looking at the clock on the mantelpiece.

As he withdrew he thought to himself that it was strange that the Duke had not explained to him at breakfast-time who his guest was.

After all, there must be a reasonable explanation for his inviting Thoreau's daughter to stay.

Yet it was unlike him to clutter himself with anyone in Paris who did not interest him in a very different manner.

It was obvious to Mr Beaumont that Una was little more than a child and obviously a lady.

The only possible reason therefore, that the Duke had invited her to his house in the Rue du Faubourg St Honoré must be out of kindness because she had lost her father.

"There is one thing about him," Mr Beaumont said, as he picked up some papers which needed his attention, "he often surprises me when I least expect it."

The Duke, riding in the unfashionable part of the Bois, enjoyed the difficulty of keeping his spirited horse under control and the warmth of the sunshine made him feel how wise he had been in coming to Paris.

He felt free and knew it was because he was away from Rose. For the moment, at any rate, it was impossible for her to quarrel with him and continue her demands that they should be married.

"One thing about Paris," the Duke said to himself, "is that one does not have to think about respectability and a woman's reputation."

He was sick to death of Rose's continual argument that he must make reparation by making an honest woman of her.

"Nothing could make her that," he told himself.

He thought that if she did become his wife, it was very unlikely that she would remain faithful to him.

As he thought of it, he knew that he had decided once and for all, that his affair with Lady Rose Caversham had come to an end.

She had, for a long time, excited, amused and entertained him, and they had definitely a physical rapport which had given him a great deal of pleasure.

But he neither loved nor respected Rose Caversham, and he thought that if he ever should marry, those were two feelings he would want to have for his wife.

Then he told himself cynically if that was the criterion that he set himself, he would doubtless remain a bachelor until his dying day.

As he rode on, his thoughts kept returning to Una.

It would be interesting, he thought, to see if she was as unusually lovely by day, as she appeared to be by night.

It was easy to be deceived after a good dinner and in the golden glamour of gaslights, into thinking that a woman was far lovelier than she was.

The Duke had seen far too many women in the early morning, when their faces were as nature had endowed them and their hair had not been attended to by an expensive hairdresser, not to be suspicious of what was called 'the finished article'.

"I shall doubtless find she is quite ordinary and somewhat bourgeoise," he told himself, as he turned for home.

At the same time, it was impossible not to acknowledge that he felt an unusual flicker of interest at the thought of seeing her again and watching her enact, with what he admitted was amazing skill, her part as the innocent virgin.

"Dubucheron has trained her well," the Duke thought for the hundredth time as he recalled what had been said the night before.

The way Una had looked, the manner in which she had managed to attract his attention without apparently making any effort to do so, had been faultless.

Then suddenly an idea struck him and he told himself he had found a flaw.

Dubucheron had been clever, but he was cleverer still.

Any really young and innocent girl, the Duke told himself, going to the Moulin Rouge for the first time, would have been shocked.

He had been looking at Una while La Goulue was dancing, and she had watched the performance with the fascinated expression of a child at a Pantomime.

But La Goulue was not the type that one was likely to find in any Pantomime that was planned for children.

The Duke had actually seen the dancer the last time he had been in Paris and had learnt a great deal about her.

Her real name was Louise Weber and her nickname, which meant 'glutton' came from her habit of sucking every last drop from glasses and also from her voracious appetite for food and sexual pleasure.

She was a genuine child of the streets and had started her career by wandering from café to café, dance-hall to dance-hall.

Her earthy sexiness and frank vulgarity had brought her fame.

Her high kicks, high spirits, and a fleeting glimpse of two inches of bare feminine flesh between her stockings and frilly knickers, had filled the Élysées Montmartre where she had danced before she went to the Moulin Rouge.

But while men enjoyed the lasciviousness of her twisting limbs and the turbulent swirl of her petticoats, any decent woman would have been disgusted at the immoral and obscene climax to her dance.

'I have caught them out!' the Duke thought with a sense of elation.

Dubucheron and his little protégée had been clever, but not clever enough.

As he neared the Faubourg St Honoré he felt really pleased with himself, but he decided he would not expose Una immediately.

Although he was not deceived by her pretence of being an innocent, she intrigued him and she was also Thoreau's daughter.

Then the Duke pulled up.

"Perhaps that too is a lie," he wondered.

Dubucheron would have remembered that he had bought a picture by Thoreau last year, and the moment he learnt he had arrived in Paris, another one was waiting.

What could have been cleverer than to provide him with a mistress who was, in some way, connected with the artist he admired?

"Dammit all!" he told himself, "I will make enquiries about Thoreau!"

He had a feeling he had been presented with one of those Chinese puzzles which most people found impossible to solve, and almost like a small boy with a new toy, he was intrigued with the idea that he would confound everyone by finding the solution.

He knew, as he dismounted from his horse, that he was looking forward to seeing Una again, but not in the same way as he sought other women, simply because they were beautiful and attracted him physically.

This was a challenge! This was where he pitted his wits against a man and a woman who had plotted to make him their victim.

Well, he would give them a run for their money! But he would also show them he was not the fool they thought him to be!

He handed his whip, gloves and top-hat to the servants in the Hall and walked towards the Salon.

A footman opened the door for him and he stepped in to the room and thought, just as Mr Beaumont had, that Una was not there.

Then she came running towards him and he saw as the sunshine shone on her face and her hair, that she was even lovelier than he remembered.

"Oh, I am so glad you have come back!" she exclaimed almost breathlessly. "I have found something exciting, so exciting that I cannot wait to tell you about it."

It was not the way the Duke had expected to be greeted, but he answered:

"You have found something? What do you mean?"

She held up what she had in her hand, and he saw it was a drawing on old, rather yellow paper.

He took it from her and as if she could not repress her excitement, Una said:

"I found it pushed away in the back of a drawer with some other sketches, and I felt certain that you could not have known it was there or you would have had it framed."

"What do you think it is?" the Duke asked seeing that the drawing was of some goddesses surrounded by small cupids.

"I am almost certain," Una said, "and perhaps you will know better than I do, that it is a study by Tiepolo for one of his famous pictures."

She pointed at it with her fingers as she went on:

"Look, you can see his style, and the way Aphrodite is sitting, the manner in which she holds her hand, and the cupids are identical to those I have seen in his other pictures."

There was so much enthusiasm and excitement in her voice that the Duke looked down at her with a smile that, for the moment, was not cynical or mocking.

He thought, as he did so, that her eyes had caught the sunshine and her skin was the perfection of a pearl which had just been taken from its oyster-shell.

Her hair was the very soft gold usually found on young children, and she had curling-back eye-lashes which were dark at the roots, deepening to gold at the tips.

Everything about her, the Duke thought, was quite different from the beauty he had found in other women, and he wondered, too, how long it was since he had heard anyone sound so enthusiastic or excited about anything except himself.

"We must certainly ascertain if you are right about this sketch," he said aloud.

"I do hope I am!" Una said. "It would be very humiliating to be found wrong."

"Would that matter?" he enquired.

"It would be so disappointing to have raised your hopes," she replied naïvely.

"My hopes?" the Duke smiled, "this is your find and therefore, if you are right, the glory will be yours."

"Perhaps it was . . . wrong of me to look in the . . . drawer," Una said suddenly, with a contrite note in her voice, "but it was such a beautiful commode and I thought, as it was in the Salon it would not matter if I peeped inside."

"I am delighted that you have done so."

"Do you mean that?"

"I am in the habit of saying what I mean," the Duke answered.

"I have . . . something to . . . suggest to you," Una said.

He raised his eye-brows as she continued, a little nervously:

"I thought when I found this sketch that perhaps the way I could . . . work for you, would be to catalogue . . . all the things you have in this . . . wonderful house. I am sure there must be heaps of treasures that have been hidden away and forgotten about, and perhaps I could find them for you."

"I think that is rather a good idea," the Duke said.

He was quite sure as he spoke, that Beaumont, who was meticulous over things of that kind, had made an inventory of everything in the house in the Faubourg St Honoré. Certainly there were inventories that were checked every year, of his houses in England and his villas abroad.

For one thing, the insurance companies insisted on it.

He doubted if Una was aware of this or perhaps she was and had been singularly astute in finding a good pretext for being in his employment.

"You shall be my Curator," he said, "and of course, we shall have to decide on the salary you will receive."

She did not speak and after a moment he asked:

"Have you any idea? Have you something in mind?"

He thought, as he spoke, that this would be a very good excuse for her either to ask for a preposterous salary, or else to say modestly that a piece of jewellery — quite a small piece, of course — would be just as acceptable!

He watched Una as she appeared to be thinking over his suggestion. Then she said:

"That is rather a difficult question to answer because I have not been living in France. But I know what the teachers who came to the Convent for special subjects received."

"And what was that?" the Duke enquired.

"Translated into francs," Una replied, "it would be about 600 francs a year."

She thought the Duke looked surprised and said quickly:

"Of course I would not expect to receive as much as that, but perhaps 300 or 400 would be fair."

This, in English money, was less than £20 a year, and although the Duke thought this was about right for a young Nursery-Governess, it was not anything like the sum a knowledgeable curator would require from him.

Aloud he said:

"Perhaps we had better leave the question of your salary for the moment. I shall, of course, be delighted for you to catalogue anything you think of value."

Una gave a little sigh!

"That means everything! I never knew a room could hold so many beautiful objects and I wish Papa could have seen your pictures."

"Do you think he would have appreciated them?"

"Of course he painted in a different manner," Una replied, "but he once said that art was like women — every man found what appealed to his particular taste among the greatest pictures in the world!"

"Did your father ever paint you?" the Duke enquired.

"When I was a very little girl," Una answered, "but he was never satisfied with his portraits. I think he preferred painting landscapes, although sometimes he put Mama in the foreground to give it what he called balance."

She spoke reminiscently, then she thought perhaps she was being rude to talk so much about herself. She asked:

"Did you enjoy your ride?"

"Very much," the Duke answered, "and it was so delightful in the Bois that I thought we would drive there in my Chaise and have luncheon in an outdoor Restaurant."

Una clasped her hands together.

"Do you . . . mean that?"

"It is an invitation."

"Can we go now . . . at once?"

"You must give me time to change from my riding-clothes," the Duke smiled, "and I think perhaps you will need a hat."

"Yes, of course," Una said. "I will go and get ready right away."

Her eyes seemed almost to glitter as she said:

"Thank you for asking me. It is the most exciting thing I could ever imagine, to have luncheon in the Bois."

She went from the room without waiting to say any more and the Duke looked after her in perplexity.

Could she really be acting a part?

Then he told himself there were many things he had been in life, but never, as far as he could remember, except on one occasion, a greenhorn who would accept what his eyes and his ears heard, without using his mind.

Nevertheless he was smiling as he went upstairs to his bedroom.

His valet helped him to change his clothes, thinking as he did so, that His Grace was certainly in a far better mood than he had been yesterday on the journey from England.

Mr Beaumont thought the same as he came from his office when the Duke descended the stairs.

"I understand you want a Chaise, Your Grace."

"I shall be out for luncheon," the Duke replied.

"And have you any plans for this evening?" Mr Beaumont enquired.

"Not at the moment," the Duke answered. "When I have I will let you know."

Mr Beaumont thought with amusement, that the Duke was determined not to be confidential and he was equally determined not to appear curious.

They were, however, saved from further conversation as Una came hurrying down the stairs.

On her head was a hat exactly the same shape as the one she had worn yesterday except that it was of plain white straw.

She had in fact, only two hats, the one in which she had travelled and which had blue ribbons around it to match her travelling-gown, and this one which she had hurriedly ornamented with a piece of pink chiffon.

She had also added a little pink silk rose which one of the girls at School had given to her as a present.

Trimming her hat had delayed her, but she felt that she must emulate in some way, what she knew would be the magnificence of the Duke's appearance.

She had not been mistaken and in his hose-pipe trousers, his well-cut morning coat and elegant waist-coat, he looked so re-splendent that she felt a little self-conscious about her own appearance.

However there was nothing else she could wear and she only hoped that perhaps he would not notice her particularly.

The Duke in fact, noticed every detail and thought once again, how clever someone had been to dress Una so skilfully for the part.

The simple flowered cotton gown had, he thought, been designed by a master-hand, and with the turned-back white straw hat which haloed her fair hair and childlike face, she might have stepped from a picture in the Academy.

Una reached the Hall.

"I hope I have not kept Your Grace waiting," she said breathlessly.

"There is no hurry," he replied, "but as it is such a lovely day, it would be a pity to waste any of it."

"A lovely, lovely day!" Una cried, "and I can drive in the Bois!"

Mr Beaumont thought that she looked the Spirit of Youth. He also thought that any other women of the Duke's acquaintance would have said it was a lovely day because she was driving with him.

He wondered if His Grace noticed the difference.

As a matter of fact, the Duke did, and as they drove away side by side, in his very elegant Chaise with a groom sitting out of earshot behind them, he said:

"Have you never been to the Bois before?"

"Not for a very long time," Una replied. "I came once with Mama to see the Aquarium, and once in the winter when there were skaters on the ice."

Her voice seemed to change as she said:

"I cannot tell you how beautiful it was. There were sleighs with beautiful women in them and fine gentlemen to push them. There was frost on the trees and snow on the ground and it all made a picture that made me long to be an artist."

"You should express what you feel in prose," the Duke suggested.

"Are you saying that I should write a book?" Una asked.

"Why not?"

"It would be an exciting thing to do," Una answered, "and perhaps would make me a little money."

The Duke's lips curved at the corners.

'Now we are getting down to it,' he thought.

But to his surprise Una changed the subject, pointing out with delight the balloon-men standing beneath the chestnut-trees as they drove up the Champs Élysées.

It was not until they were sitting at luncheon in one of the crowded but fashionable Restaurants in the Bois that he had a chance to test her.

He had a feeling to which he was not at all accustomed, that he was barely holding her attention, when she was so interested in everything that was happening around her.

The tables were set in the garden of the Restaurant; there was a small lake in front of them and trees covered in blossom overhead.

The food was superlative and Una kept hoping she would remember the dishes so that she could try to prepare them herself.

Then she remembered a little wistfully that she had no-one to prepare them for. She was sure, if she suggested cooking a meal for the Duke, his Chef would be horrified.

He might even give notice, she told herself, and that would annoy the Duke more than anything else.

"There is something I want to ask you," the Duke said, as he saw that Una's eyes were on the white swans moving majestically over the smooth water of the lake.

"What is it?" she asked.

"I was wondering," he said, "what you thought last night when you saw La Goulue dance. Surely her performance somewhat surprised you?"

Una did not answer for a moment and the Duke thought he had embarrassed her.

"I was right," he told himself. "Neither Dubucheron nor this girl had thought I would notice that she was not shocked and

158

did not even make a presence of looking away from such an exhibition."

He wondered how she would get out of the impasse into which he had thrown her, by one simple question.

With his eyes on her face, he waited thinking again, because he could not help it, that she certainly looked the part she wished to convey.

"Papa always told me," Una said after a moment, "that there was nothing wrong in nakedness. 'It is natural,' he said, 'and only people with vulgar minds would find anything that was not beautiful in the pictures of Aphrodite or the statues of Venus'."

"I agree," the Duke said, "but I want to know what you thought about La Goulue."

"I felt a little . . . embarrassed at first by the . . . manner in which she danced," Una replied. "Then I thought it was like pictures made by primitive people which seem crude and rough to us, but were in fact, drawn by artists striving towards some ideal of beauty that was achieved by Michaelangelo or Botticelli."

The Duke was listening attentively.

"Go on," he said.

"The primitives did their best, just as those very early murals on caves and catacombs were the efforts of men who could only draw what they were capable of depicting."

"Are you saying that La Goulue's dancing was primitive, and yet the best of which she was capable?" the Duke enquired.

"Perhaps I am explaining myself badly," Una said a little helplessly, "but while I, and I expect you, would rather watch a beautiful ballet like Les Sylphides, that woman last night was dancing, striving perhaps towards something she could never attain, but knows it would be the perfection of her art."

The Duke was astounded.

He had never imagined anyone could put that type of interpretation on the deliberate voluptuousness of La Goulue's performance.

Then he asked sharply:

"Who told you to say that. Was it Dubucheron?"

Una looked at him in astonishment.

"No . . . of course not! You know I did not get a chance to talk to Monsieur Dubucheron because we left so early. Anyway, it is just what I feel myself. Is it wrong?"

There was anxiety in the last question and Una's eyes searched the Duke's face as if she was afraid she would see an expression of disapproval in them.

"No, not wrong," the Duke said slowly,

"but I was frankly surprised that you were not more shocked by what you saw."

"If I had been . . . if it was . . . meant to be . . . shocking," Una said, "would . . . you have taken . . . me there?"

This, the Duke thought, was certainly putting the ball back in his court, and he said quickly:

"I had decided to go to the Moulin Rouge before I met you."

"I am glad I have been there," Una remarked, "but I would not wish to go again."

"Why not?"

"I knew even when I went there, that Mama would not have . . . approved. I had always understood that it was a place for gentlemen to enjoy by themselves."

"I am afraid there are a lot of places like that in Paris," the Duke said, "and I hope you do not intend to say that you will not visit them with me."

"I should be . . . glad to go with you . . . anywhere you suggest," Una answered, "but you did not really . . . like La Goulue's dancing, did you?"

"Why do you ask me that?" the Duke asked.

"Because I feel that you really like the beautiful things around you. No-one could live with the Fragonards and the Bouchers

on your walls and the pictures in your
Dining Room without comparing them to
the posters outside the Moulin Rouge."

"You noticed them?" the Duke asked.

"Yes . . . while we were waiting for the
carriage."

"And you realised who drew them?"

She nodded.

"Toulouse-Lautrec, and when I saw him,
I understood how he could draw only those
crude, but very, very clever posters."

"You think a man expresses himself in
what he paints?"

As he spoke, Una saw the picture that had
stood on the easel in her father's Studio.

That had been himself — that had been
what he was like before he died.

She shrank away from the thought of it, as
if from something foul and evil.

The Duke saw the expression on her face
and did not understand it.

"I am worrying her," he told himself, and
thought again that she had an unusual intel-
ligence for a woman, let alone one so young.

Then he was sure that Dubucheron was
behind it. He had trained her and taught
her. He would be a fool to think for a
moment that a girl of nineteen or whatever
she said she was, could talk as they were
talking now.

And yet, at the same time, he wondered in fact, if such a lunch-time conversation was likely to take place with any man except himself.

He knew that nearly all his contemporaries who came to Paris for a little fun, would, by this time, be making love to her.

They would expect her to amuse them with a witty *double entendre* and the light, frothy laughter which was characteristic of a young *demi-mondaine*.

It seemed to the Duke that the Chinese puzzle he was attempting to unravel, was not as easy as he had first thought and he decided he would try another tactic.

"What would you like to do this afternoon?" he asked.

"Could we go on . . . driving in your . . . Chaise?" she asked. "It is so exciting to be behind such magnificent horses, and to see Paris in a way I never expected I could do."

"You have omitted something rather important," the Duke said.

"What is that?" she asked.

"You have not mentioned the person who will be driving."

"Do you mean . . . you?"

"I am feeling somewhat neglected."

She laughed.

"What does Your Grace want me to say?

163

That you drive better than any man I have ever seen? You are so kind to me that I feel as if I am in a dream. I am just praying you will not find me a bore too quickly."

"I was rather afraid you had forgotten my existence," the Duke said.

She laughed again.

"How could I possibly do that? I keep thinking that it is all so wonderful that suddenly I shall wake up to find I am back in the Convent."

The Duke's eyes twinkled.

"I am rather suspicious of that Convent."

"Suspicious?" Una asked.

"I always imagined that girls who came straight from School were too shy to speak, and fat and dumpy from all the good, wholesome food they had been eating."

"I was shy when I first saw you," Una said impulsively.

"Why?"

"I do not know," she replied. "I am never shy as a rule. Perhaps it was because I have not met many distinguished people . . . but I do not think it was that."

"Then what was it?" he prompted.

"Perhaps because you seemed so . . . magnificent," Una said slowly, "but I think it was something else as well."

"Tell me," the Duke said.

"Everyone gives out a certain . . . vibration," Una explained, "and I can feel at once, if they are nice . . . and pleasant . . . But sometimes they are rather nondescript . . . and one is not . . . interested."

"And my vibrations?" the Duke questioned.

"I felt they were . . . different from . . . anyone else's."

She looked up into his eyes and said with a little cry:

"I know you will think I am talking a lot of nonsense! Why do you make me talk about myself, when I want to talk about you and Paris?"

"Which comes first?" the Duke asked.

"It would be very impolite to say Paris!"

He laughed.

"I cannot make up my mind about you," he said. "I keep feeling you are too good to be true."

He saw she did not understand, and because he did not wish to alert her in any way, to what his real feelings were, he said:

"Come, I will show you Paris and to tell the truth, I rather enjoy driving these horses which I borrowed from a friend. My own will be arriving tomorrow, or the next day."

"You are bringing your horses to Paris?"

"I seldom go anywhere without them."

"How wonderful!" Una exclaimed. Then she added: "I suppose that is being really . . . rich."

She thought for a moment, then she went on:

"Having so many possessions must be in some ways, extremely thrilling, but supposing they are not enough?"

"What do you mean by that?" the Duke asked.

"I think I am very . . . ignorant in many of the things I say," Una answered, "but I have read a lot and it has always appeared to me that men feel the need of a challenge."

The Duke's eyes were surprised but he did not speak.

"Men want to do things to achieve things, to be a victor, a conqueror. Then they become heroes whom other men want to emulate."

Una spoke almost as if she was speaking to herself and the Duke thought in a cynical manner, when he replied, that he had asked the same question of Mr Beaumont.

"What are you suggesting I do?"

"I do not know you well enough to answer that question," Una answered, "but because you are so strong and have such vital vibrations, I feel you could be like Jason who sought the Golden Fleece, Hercules wrestling with his Labours, or perhaps Sir Galahad in search of the Holy Grail."

There was something about the way she spoke which made it impossible for the Duke to laugh. Instead he said:

"You are certainly surprising me. At the same time, I feel flattered that you should think I am capable of such achievements. But now I think we should go."

Una looked round her and realised that the people who had filled all the tables when they arrived had nearly all left.

The ladies with their feathers and jewels and the gentlemen who had been talking earnestly to them, as she had been talking to the Duke, had all driven away.

She got up quickly.

"Ought . . . I to have . . . suggested we should . . . leave?" she asked, feeling she might have made a social error.

"No," the Duke said. "On such occasions it is something we agree together."

He saw the relief in Una's face and did not say anything until they were driving away from the Restaurant through the beautiful parts of the Bois that had been laid out by Baron Hausseman.

Then she said:

"When you are kind enough to take me with you anywhere, Your Grace, will you please tell me how I should behave. I am so afraid of making a *faux pas*."

"You have not made one so far," the Duke assured her.

"I have never been in any fashionable places before, and of course, never with a man . . . like you."

"What men have you been with?" he asked quickly.

"I am afraid I have never known many," Una answered. "There was Papa, of course, and the gentlemen who used to come to our house when we lived in the country. There was the Priest who heard the confessions of the girls and said Mass at the Convent every Sunday!"

She thought before she went on:

"There was the Doctor who was an Italian, who used to pretend to scold me because I was never ill, and there was a Music Master."

"What was he like?" the Duke asked. "I have heard about Music Masters before now."

"He was very, very old," Una answered, "but he had once played in a famous Orchestra."

She smiled as she continued:

"The girls who did not want to learn and found it a bore, used to inveigle him into talking about the old days, and then the lesson was over and they had not played a note."

"Did you do that?" the Duke asked.

"No. I was anxious to learn although I shall never be a good pianist."

"You were talking about the men you knew," the Duke prompted.

"I am afraid that is all," Una said, "unless of course, you count Monsieur Dubucheron and you."

"Do you expect me to believe that?" the Duke enquired.

"I do not . . . think I have forgotten anyone," Una replied. "Of course, there was the postman and the gardeners at the Convent, and the gendarmes who used to hold up the traffic for us when we crossed the road to visit the Galleries. They used to wink at the older girls and the Nuns would get very angry."

"She *is* too good to be true," the Duke repeated beneath his breath.

He felt, as he did so, that Una was beginning to mesmerise him.

"If this goes on," he told himself, "I shall believe the whole fairy-story from the start to the finish."

He drove his horses for some moments without speaking, then looked sideways to see if she was waiting for him to continue their conversation.

To his surprise she was staring with delight at the places they were passing and apparently not in the least perturbed that she had lost his attention.

To his astonishment he felt quite piqued.

"Where would you like to dine tonight?" he asked and Una's face turned to him.

"Dine?" she asked. "Do you mean in a Restaurant?"

"Why not?" he asked. "I think you would find it interesting, and of course, I would like to show off the very beautiful lady I have accompanying me."

"You intend to ask Mademoiselle Joyant to be your guest?" Una enquired.

The Duke gave her a quick glance before he replied:

"I was intending we should dine alone."

There was silence, then Una said:

"I would love that, but I am afraid you will not be particularly proud of me this evening, for I have only the evening-gown which I wore last night."

The Duke's eyes twinkled.

Here it came at last! Here was the breakthrough he had been waiting for.

"Well, that is easily remedied," he said. "If your wardrobe is so limited, then we must do something about it."

"What . . . do you . . . mean?"

"I mean," he replied, "that of course, you must choose some gowns — any gowns that take your fancy, and I will pay the bill."

He spoke bluntly because he thought they had played games for long enough. The sooner they got down to fundamentals the better.

There was silence and because she did not speak for so long, the Duke turned once again to look at the little face raised to his.

"What is it?" he asked.

"I do not . . . think I . . . understand," Una replied. "Are you . . . suggesting that you should give me . . . a gown?"

"As many as you like," the Duke said carelessly. "You need not be afraid of bank-rupting me."

"I am sure . . . you mean to be very . . . kind," she said in a hesitating little voice, "and it is very . . . generous of you . . . but I could not accept a gown as a present, and it will be . . . some time before I could earn enough to pay for them myself."

The Duke hesitated as to whether he should say: 'Stop pretending!' Then he told himself she might as well continue the farce of deceiving him.

But he could not help supposing that she

thought, by doing so, the rewards would be very much greater, than if she succumbed too quickly.

Instead he merely said:

"You are not very grateful for a present I wish to give you."

"I am not . . . being ungrateful," Una said, "and as I have said . . . you are very, very kind . . . but it would not be right . . . and so I can only say . . . thank you again . . . but no."

"Why?" the Duke asked. "I do not understand."

"Mama always told me," Una said, "that a lady could never accept any present from a gentleman."

The Duke thought of all the dozens of women who had accepted with alacrity anything he was pleased to give them.

It always started with a small jewel, a brooch, a bracelet, a pair of ear-rings, then it escalated towards pearls which cost an enormous sum, then gowns, furs, as well as sunshades and a thousand other things.

He did not, for a moment, believe that Una intended to refuse his offer: she was merely expecting him to overrule her objections.

"I think the sensible thing to do," he said, "would be to send for one of the famous

Couturiers from the Rue de la Paix, and suggest he design things that will express your personality and your originality. He will, in the meantime, provide you with something to wear until they are ready."

Una clenched her hands together.

"I shall be able to . . . buy myself a new gown when Monsieur Dubucheron pays me for Papa's picture."

The Duke gave a short laugh.

"That is a very impractical suggestion and not one I should have thought you were so foolish as to make."

"Foolish?"

"You know as well as I do, any money you get from your father's picture or anything you earn, must be kept against a rainy day. It always comes sooner or later! In the meantime, I am ready to be your banker and you should not refuse my offer."

"I have tried to . . . explain to you," Una said, "it would not be . . . right. Mama said that if one was engaged to a gentleman, it was permissible for him to give his fiancée a fan or even a pair of gloves at Christmas, but anything else would be misconstrued by everyone who learnt about it."

"Misconstrued? In what way?" the Duke asked slowly.

Una paused, then she said hesitatingly:

"Mama thought that a girl would be considered very . . . fast to allow a gentleman, however well she knew him, to give her an article of clothing."

"If your mother thought that was fast," the Duke said, "what do you think she would say about you staying alone in my house, without a chaperon?"

There was a silence, then Una said slowly:

"I never thought about it . . . until this moment. Was it . . . wrong of me to . . . accept your invitation? I had nowhere . . . else to go."

There was a little touch of panic in her voice and the Duke said:

"Personally I should have thought it extremely stupid to have refused my invitation, and be forced to look for lodgings in the middle of the night."

"It would have been . . . very frightening."

"Having swallowed a camel," the Duke said, "why strain at a gnat?"

"You mean . . . that as I am . . . staying at your house . . . I should allow you to give me a gown?"

"Not one gown, but all that you need."

Una was silent for a moment, then she said:

"Please . . . may I think about . . . it?"

"Of course," he replied. "Take your time

174

and perhaps we could go somewhere quiet tonight, so that I need not be ashamed of you."

He thought as he spoke, he was breaking all the Queensberry Rules and hitting below the belt. At the same time, he was beginning to find the conversation rather boring.

He wanted to dress Una.

He wanted her to look as beautiful as he knew she could look in one of the exquisite gowns that were created in Paris, and copied by every fashionable woman in the world.

"Dammit all!" he said to himself. "It is about time I took the lead in this drama which could only be happening in Paris but should have been written for French and not English actors."

5

They drove on for some way before the Duke spoke again. Then he asked:

"What is your favourite stone?"

Una, who had obviously been thinking of something else, seemed to start at his voice.

"Stone?"

"I mean jewel," the Duke explained. "All women love jewellery. I do not suppose that you are an exception."

Una thought for a moment, then she said:

"I think turquoises are very beautiful and I expect you know that in the East they are considered to be lucky."

"I have heard that," the Duke said.

"Mama said the Tibetans who mine stones in the mountains always wear a piece of turquoise to keep away the 'Evil Eye'."

She gave a little laugh.

"I do not suppose you are afraid of the 'Evil Eye', but in the books I have read it was a very real menace in mediaeval times."

The Duke realised that once again she was moving away from the subject he wished to discuss.

"So if you had the choice, you would rather own a turquoise than any other gem?"

"I expect I should feel very lucky if I had one," Una replied, "but as I was born in July, I believe my birthstone is a ruby."

The Duke smiled to himself.

This was getting better. Now she was beginning to show her interest in the expensive jewels which he was quite certain she would end up by demanding.

"At the same time," Una went on, "I think rubies are rather sinister and perhaps the best and most lovely jewel of all is a pearl."

"Pearls can be very expensive," the Duke said.

"I am sure all jewels are," she replied, "which is why I am very unlikely ever to own any."

She gave a little sigh.

"Mama said that what she minded selling more than anything else, when she and Papa came to France, was the diamond crescent which her mother had left her in her will."

The Duke knew that diamond crescents and diamond stars were very fashionable amongst English women, but he had always thought himself, that the jewellery which could be bought in Paris was the finest in the world.

His mother had worn a tiara set by Oscar Massin which he suddenly thought would look extremely attractive, young though she was, upon Una.

Massin was a master-craftsman who created jewelled flowers with ears of corn, sprays of eglantine and lilies-of-the-valley.

His lilies-of-the-valley, the Duke told himself, might have been especially fashioned for Una.

Although it was absurd to imagine she would ever wear anything from the Wolstanton collection, he thought perhaps he would buy her a brooch made of diamond lilies-of-the-valley.

Also, if she insisted, he would add a pearl necklace that would encircle her small round neck and enhance the beauty of her skin.

Aloud he said:

"What you are really saying is that you would rather own pearls than anything else."

"I know what I would rather have more than all the jewels in the world," Una replied.

"What is that?" he asked curiously.

"Horses like the ones you are driving now

and are the equal, I am sure, of those you possess yourself."

The Duke was astonished.

Once again he had been unable to hold her attention, as would have been very easy with any other woman, on the irresistible subject of what he should give her.

"If you had a horse where would you keep it?" he asked.

Una laughed light-heartedly.

"I could hardly expect you to invite it to stay, as you invited me, and I am afraid I should get into trouble if I let it graze unattended in the Bois!"

She was making it all a fairy-story and as the Duke thought what he could reply, she went on:

"Perhaps really one should have an invisible horse, or at least, invisible until one was riding it."

"It would certainly save a lot of trouble," the Duke agreed, feeling he should enter into her fantasy.

"I always thought it was very unfair that the Immortals and the Witches had so many things, which one would love to have oneself."

"What sort of things?" the Duke asked.

"A magic mirror on the wall for one," Una replied, "to tell the true character of the person who looked into it."

"I thought you were telling me just now, that you could do that without the aid of a magic mirror," the Duke answered.

"Perhaps it is . . . presumptuous of me," she said, "but I can . . . sometimes be aware, not only of people's . . . personalities but also what is . . . happening in their lives."

"You are a fortune-teller?" the Duke asked scornfully.

"Not exactly."

"And have you had any prognostications about me?"

She hesitated for a moment. Then she said:

"Perhaps you would . . . rather not hear."

"I not only want to hear, but I insist on hearing," the Duke said. "If you make such ambiguous remarks, you can hardly expect me to ignore them."

"Well, I thought last night at dinner," Una said, "that you talked and listened to what was being said. At the same time, you were . . . watching, not really . . . participating."

The Duke did not speak and she gave a little cry.

"Once again I am explaining myself badly, but it was as if everyone around you was on the stage and you were in the audience."

"I am not going to tell you if that is correct," the Duke answered, "but I would like to hear what else you thought."

He was sure, as he spoke, that doubtless Dubucheron, who was a very keen judge of men, had given her a short outline of his character before they arrived for dinner.

Now Una hesitated longer than she had before, then said in a very low voice:

"I may be quite wrong . . . I think perhaps I am . . . but I have a feeling . . . you are trying to . . . make up your mind about . . . yourself."

She looked away from him after she had spoken.

He knew suddenly she felt not exactly shy, but self-conscious because she was speaking of something which came from deep inside her.

It was astounding but he thought it would be a mistake to say so, and he merely replied lightly:

"You are not making it very clear."

"It is not very clear to me," Una said, "but perhaps it is . . . something that is . . . going to happen. I can sometimes see things . . . out of time."

"Out of time?" the Duke questioned.

Una smiled.

"Papa said once, that if we were high

enough up in the sky, we could see Cherbourg, New York, and a ship in the Atlantic."

She glanced at the Duke from under her eye-lashes as if afraid she was boring him, but seeing he was listening, she went on:

"The people on board the ship would believe they had left Cherbourg yesterday, that where they were at the moment in the middle of the ocean was today, and New York was several days ahead."

"I see what you mean," the Duke said slowly. "For you and me high up in the sky it would all be happening at the same moment."

Una smiled at him as if he had been rather clever.

"Exactly!" she said, "and that is why I sometimes feel, when I am very interested in a person, that I can see a little bit of his or her yesterdays and tomorrows, while it is happening to me today."

"And you are very interested in me?" the Duke asked.

"Of course," she answered. "I think you are the most complicated . . . difficult . . . and of course, much the most . . . exciting person I have ever looked at in my magic mirror."

She laughed as she spoke and the Duke smiled.

"You are making me nervous," he said. "Suppose you find out I am really a wicked ogre in disguise? What will you do then?"

She did not say that was impossible, she merely replied:

"I should slip on my invisible dancing shoes which would carry me seven leagues away before you knew what was happening! I might even put a spell on you!"

The Duke thought they had journeyed a long way from his original enquiry as to what stones she favoured.

Now in fact, they were back in the Rue du Faubourg St Honoré and their drive was over.

He suddenly decided the best way to deal with anyone as elusive as Una, was to present her with a *fait accompli*.

He decided that instead of taking her to Oscar Massin's shop as he had intended, he would go alone, buy her a present, then see how she behaved when he offered it to her.

Accordingly, as they alighted, he told the servants to keep his Chaise and followed Una into the Hall.

The Clerk-of-the-Chambers came forward to say:

"There's a gentleman to see Your Grace. I've put him in the Ante-chamber."

The Duke guessed that his visitor would

be Dubucheron with Thoreau's pictures which he had undoubtedly collected by now from Montmartre.

He hesitated for a moment, as to whether he should take Una with him to inspect them, then decided he would rather see them himself first.

But while he was trying to make up his mind Una had started up the stairs.

The Duke, therefore, without speaking walked away down the passage which led to the Ante-chamber where he usually saw dealers like Dubucheron, with something to sell.

As he went, he decided that he would certainly take the opportunity of finding out more about Una, though he was quite convinced that Dubucheron would try to be mysterious about her and her past.

Una was half-way up the staircase when a sudden thought came to her.

For a moment she stood indecisive, then she ran back down the stairs and into the Hall.

"I want a *fiacre*," she said to one of the footmen.

The servant looked surprised, but it was not his job to question anything the Gentry might wish to do and he ran through the courtyard and out into the street to return within a few seconds, with an open *fiacre* drawn by a thin, rather tired horse.

He opened the door and Una stepped into it.

"Where to, M'mselle?"

"Please ask him to go to No. 9, Rue de l'Abreuville."

The footman gave the order to the Cocher, and they drove off.

Only when they had driven for quite a little way, did Una wonder whether she should have left a message to tell the Duke where she was going.

It had suddenly struck her that as Monsieur Dubuchcron had obtained a large sum of money from the Duke for her father's picture, there might be others in the Studio which could also be sold.

She had a feeling the Duke was going to be difficult about letting her spend the money he was paying for the picture he had bought.

But if there were other purchasers of her father's pictures, that money would pay for a new evening-gown, so that the Duke would not be ashamed of her.

She realised she had annoyed him in refusing to allow him to buy her new clothes as he had offered to do.

She was quite certain, whatever he might say, that her mother would think it exceedingly reprehensible for her to accept expensive presents, not only from a gentleman but from one she had only just met.

Her mother had been very proud and she had taught Una there was no crime in being poor. It was wrong only when people pretended to be different from what they were.

This meant, she explained, lowering their self-esteem and accepting favours which they could not possibly return.

Una remembered once hearing her mother argue with her father over some rich Americans to whom he had sold a picture and who subsequently wished to entertain them.

"We cannot ask them back here," her mother had said, "and therefore, Julius, I have no desire to accept their hospitality."

"That is a ridiculous attitude!" her father exclaimed. "They are rich enough to wine and dine half Paris."

"And half Paris will accept!" her mother said quickly, "and that is exactly why we will refuse their invitation courteously but firmly."

"It is all very well to give yourself airs and graces!" her father retorted, "but quite frankly I should have enjoyed a dinner where expense was no object and the wine would undoubtedly be superlative."

Her mother had not continued to argue about it, but Una remembered that neither she nor her father had gone to the Americans' party.

Afterwards she had said to her mother:

"What a pity you did not go, Mama. It would have been a chance for you to wear one of your evening-gowns which you have not worn for many years."

Her mother had smiled.

"They are out of fashion now, dearest, and I have no wish to be beholden to anyone, certainly not the type of people my father would not have had inside his house."

As Una grew older, she began to understand the pride which could not accept, unless one could give in return.

She knew now that her mother would think she was humiliating herself, if she allowed the Duke, kind though he was, to pay for her clothes.

"I must learn to stand on my own feet," she said. "There must be some way, I can make enough money quickly, so that I can have a new gown, if not for tonight, then for tomorrow."

She remembered there were lots of small dressmakers in the side-streets of Paris, who could copy the most elaborate clothes that came from what the Duke had called 'the famous Couturiers'.

"If I can sell one of Papa's pictures," Una planned, "then I could have a lovely new gown and the Duke will not only be surprised, but will admire me in it."

She thought, a little wistfully, that she wanted him to admire her, she wanted him to think that she looked pretty.

Then as she thought of Yvette Joyant and the ladies they had seen sitting in the Restaurant in the Bois, she felt her spirits sink.

How could she ever look as smart as they? Besides she was certain that their gowns had, in fact, cost more than she could earn in years and years.

One blessing however, she told herself, was that she had a very tiny waist.

This was the fashion above full skirts which trailed on the ground at the back and gave a woman, as she stepped into a room, the grace of a swan gliding over the lake.

"There was no-one in the Restaurant as handsome as the Duke," Una told herself, thinking of where they had had luncheon.

She thought how kind he had been to take her there when doubtless he would rather have been talking to one of the ladies with feathers in their hats, which they wore on exquisitely coiffured heads.

It seemed to Una that she had set herself an impossible task in seeking to copy any of those women and yet, she told herself, she had to try.

"Help me, Mama," she whispered in her heart. "Help me to do what is right and what you would want me to do, and still please the Duke."

She had the feeling that it was going to be difficult to compromise between the two people who, at the moment, filled her whole thoughts to the exclusion of everyone else.

Then she saw Sacré Cœur looming up above her and she ceased to think of herself in the excitement of being in Montmartre again.

The horse climbed very, very slowly up the steep hill. Then there were the artists in their velvet suits, working at their easels, at every corner, in doorways and, as she had seen them before, in the Square under the trees.

A moment later, they arrived at the Rue de l'Abreuville, and the house where her father had had his Studio looked even dirtier and more dilapidated than it had yesterday.

"Will you please wait?" Una asked the Cocher.

He nodded, obviously thinking he had a rich fare seeing where he had picked her up, and Una hurried across the pavement and in through the open door.

She climbed up the dirty staircase to her father's Studio and went in.

The first thing she noticed was that some clearing up had been done since the previous day.

Quite a lot of the junk which had been littered all over the room had been brushed to one side.

Then as she turned her head, she saw an enormous mountain of rubbish piled in a corner, although there was still a large number of things to add to it.

"Where have you come from?" a voice asked.

Una jumped, not realising there was anyone else in the Studio.

Then from behind the easel which had hidden him, a man appeared and she saw that he was an artist.

It was obvious from the blue smock he was wearing smeared with paint, and above a large floppy black tie she saw the face of a young man, with a shock of long, untidy hair.

He had a palette in one hand and a paintbrush in the other.

"Have you . . . taken over this . . . Studio?" Una asked in reply to his question.

"I moved in this morning," he answered, "and a devil of a mess it's in!"

Una was just about to tell him that the mess had been made by her father but thought the information might make him embarrassed, so instead she said:

"I had no idea that anyone was here. I came to see if there were any pictures left by the previous owner."

"They have already gone," the artist replied.

"Gone?" Una repeated, almost stupidly.

"Two men came and collected them this morning," the artist explained. "I think one of them was a dealer."

"Monsieur Dubucheron?" Una enquired.

"That may have been his name, but as he was not interested in me, I saw no reason to be curious about him."

The artist spoke resentfully and Una thought sympathetically that obviously Monsieur Dubucheron did not think his pictures were saleable.

It was however, a blow to think that Monsieur Dubucheron had been here before her, and if her father had left any canvasses, he would sell them for her and doubtless the Duke would say that she was not to spend the money.

She glanced towards the great pile of rubbish, wondering if there was anything there of any value, and was not aware that the artist was watching her.

Then he said:

"You are very pretty! Not the type that one expects to find in Montmartre."

Una gave him a vague little smile.

She was still wondering whether it would be worth while to search among the dirty, dusty debris for something to sell.

"Have you done any modelling?" the artist asked.

Una's eyes widened.

Here was an idea she had not thought of before.

She had heard that artists used models and, as she had told the Duke, her father had sometimes made her mother pose for him, but it had never struck her that it was something she might do.

"Are models paid?" she asked tentatively.

"You can bet they see to that!" the artist answered. "They pick and choose who they'll sit for, as if they were prima donnas."

He spoke almost savagely, as if he had had trouble with his models, and Una said:

"Can you . . . tell me what they are . . . paid?"

His eyes narrowed and she thought he was looking at her speculatively as if he saw her now in a different way. "If you'll sit for me," he said, after a moment, "I'll pay you double what I paid the little hag who has left me for someone she thinks more important."

He smiled as he added:

"I hardly think you'd do a dirty trick like that."

"No . . . of course not," Una said. "Is your picture only half-finished?"

"Come and see for yourself," he suggested.

She walked towards him, hoping as she did so, that his picture would not look like the one of her father's which she had hated.

When she saw it on the easel, it was however, quite different from anything that Julius Thoreau had ever done, when she had lived with him.

She stared at the canvas on the easel, and said:

"I think . . . although I am not sure . . . that you are an Impressionist."

"I am," he replied, "and exceedingly proud of it, despite the fact that the newspapers say we are anarchists, madmen and unscrupulous adventurers who want to bluff the public."

"And have been described," Una added, "as the enemies of the 'purity' of French art."

"They say anything that comes into their heads," the young artist said savagely. "What annoys everyone is that we are *different*."

Una knew this was true and she had always thought it was ridiculous for anyone to say there was a 'correct' way of painting a tree, a field or a stream.

Her father painted differently from the pictures that she had seen in the Art Galleries and she knew that the great pioneers of Impressionism had a fresh vision of everything they saw.

She told herself that what she had studied in the famous Galleries in Florence had not really given her an insight into Impressionism.

However, she could not help feeling that this artist's effort had not the master-touch which she could recognise in all paintings from whatever period they came.

Impressionists, she understood, gave a new light and life to their pictures, but the canvas which stood on the easel seemed not only lifeless but to be blurred.

But there was, she saw, a vague outline of a woman in the foreground which had not yet been filled with any detail.

As if she had asked the question, the artist said:

"I scrubbed out what I had done already. I wouldn't have that woman back now, if she came and asked me on her bended knees!"

"She must have made you very angry."

"She did," he answered, "but that is women for you."

"Not all of them, I hope," Una replied, "and I do understand that it is annoying to lose your model when the picture is there in your mind."

She knew that artists, once they got started, usually worked as her father had, oblivious of time, fatigue or hunger, while he had the vision in front of him of what he wanted to convey.

"I had much better start again," the artist said gloomily. "It is always a mistake to try to complete a picture which one has started in one place and then moved to another."

"You had another Studio in Montmartre?" Una asked.

"I had a corner of one," he replied. "I was kicked out of it this morning. That is why I came here."

He looked back at the mess behind them.

"It's pretty ghastly here until I can clean it

up, but that needn't worry you. There is a bed-room up those stairs, where you can take off your clothes."

"T-take off my . . . clothes?" Una asked in a voice that seemed to die in her throat.

"Yes. Hurry up and get on with it!" he said. "The light will be going soon."

"B-but . . . but I could not!" Una said. "I . . . I mean . . . I thought I could . . . model for you . . . just as . . . I am."

The artist was already looking at his canvas.

"No," he said briefly. "I will paint you as a nymph coming from the wood. I can see it quite clearly. Hurry up!"

Una drew in her breath.

"I . . . I am . . . sorry . . . very sorry," she said, "if . . . I misled you . . . but I am afraid I . . . cannot stay now."

He turned from his easel and she saw an expression of anger in his eyes that was suddenly replaced by something else.

"Playing hard-to-get?" he asked, "or have you come here for a very different reason?"

There was something in the way he asked the question which made Una feel frightened.

"I am . . . sorry . . . very sorry," she said quickly, "b-but I have to . . . go-go . . . I have . . ."

The words died away on her lips, for the painter threw down his palette and took a step towards her.

"I said you were pretty," he said, "and now I know what your little game is. Well, the painting can wait!"

He put out his hands towards her and suddenly Una was terrified.

"No, no!" she said, backing away from him.

With a smile on his lips, he followed her.

"No!" she cried again.

He gave a laugh which was almost a shout, as he said:

"If you want a chase that's what you'll have! And when I've undressed you, you'll look exactly as I want you to look. There's nothing like combining business with pleasure!"

He spoke in a manner which made Una know that he threatened her with something so horrible, so terrible, that for a moment she thought it was impossible to move, impossible to cry out.

Then as he caught hold of her, she screamed, pulled herself free and rushed towards the door.

"You can't escape!" he shouted.

As Una screamed again, through the door she had left ajar came a man and as she

197

flung herself in sheer terror against him, she found it was the Duke!

The Duke entered the Ante-room to find, as he had expected, that Philippe Dubucheron was there, with a pile of half-a-dozen canvasses.

He had a smile on his lips which annoyed the Duke immensely, knowing that the Frenchman was thinking of how well his plans were working out and that he had found Una as delectable as he had anticipated.

As the footman shut the door, the Duke made no effort to shake hands with the Frenchman but walked across the room towards the canvasses which were stacked against the side of a chair.

"You have found some more of Thoreau's pictures?" he asked.

"Yes, Your Grace. I am afraid the majority of them are only rough sketches, but interesting, most of them showing the promise that he undoubtedly achieved with his later efforts."

Philippe Dubucheron had no intention of telling the Duke about the picture that Julius Thoreau had been working on when he died and which was at this moment waiting in his Gallery to be burnt.

He had recognised, as Una had, that it was the meandering of a drunkard's mind which had made his brush run wild in a travesty of colour, that was unpleasantly revealing.

The Duke waited and Philippe Dubucheron, wondering if anything had gone wrong, picked up the canvasses from the floor and propped them on the sofa where they were in a good light from the window.

There was only one which interested the Duke, who saw at once that it was a half-finished picture of Una as a child.

He could understand why she had said her father had not been pleased with it, but there was no mistaking who was portrayed.

In the background there was a small, rather attractive house which he supposed, must have been her home.

It struck him immediately, that one of his suspicions was unfounded.

Una undoubtedly was Thoreau's daughter and he stared at the picture for some time, wondering, as he did so, what else she had told him was the truth, and if, in fact, he had misjudged her from the very beginning.

Then there was something in the attitude of Philippe Dubucheron, the smile on his lips, and what the Duke was sure was a glint of greed in his eyes that made him certain, once again, that a trap had been set for him.

"It is not a very impressive collection," he said aloud.

He had assumed automatically the aloof, cold authority that was habitual when he was in the presence of people whom he disliked or wished to assert himself.

It made him seem very different, Dubucheron thought, from the genial host of last night or the man who had carried Una off from the Moulin Rouge and left him the unpleasant task of placating a very angry Yvette Joyant.

"I am afraid this is all I could find in Julius Thoreau's Studio, Your Grace," he replied, "although there may be more of his pictures lying about in Montmartre. It will just take time to find them."

He thought, as he spoke, that this was very unlikely. At the same time, he had to keep the Duke's interest alive. He was also avid with curiosity about Una.

Realising the Duke's eyes had lingered on the canvas that depicted her as a child, he said:

"Perhaps Miss Thoreau will know if any of her father's pictures were put in store after her mother died. It was when she was sent to school in Florence that her father sold the house in the country and moved to Montmartre."

"I gather she has not seen him since," the Duke answered, "so it is unlikely that she will know what he did in her absence."

"That is true," Philippe Dubucheron admitted. "At the same time, we could always ask her."

"Yes, we could ask her," the Duke agreed.

He thought a moment before he said:

"You told me that you yourself met Miss Thoreau only yesterday when she arrived in Paris and learnt that her father was dead."

"That is correct," Philippe Dubucheron replied.

He wondered what the Duke was getting at, and for the first time, understood that he was suspicious, though for what reason he had no idea.

"It was exceedingly fortunate that you should have been there at exactly the right moment!" the Duke continued.

"Very fortunate indeed for the young lady," Philippe Dubucheron answered. "Your Grace knows as well as I do, that someone so pretty, especially in Montmartre, could have got into all sorts of trouble."

The Duke made a sound of agreement.

"The many stories about the young artists, especially the Impressionists," Philippe Dubucheron went on, "are not unfounded. Their morals and their drinking habits are getting art a bad name, which makes it exceedingly difficult to sell their pictures or those of any other modern painter."

"I am sure you manage," the Duke said coldly.

Philippe Dubucheron made an expressive gesture with his hands.

"As Your Grace says, I manage, but then I am all things to all men. And that obviously raises the question of whether I can help Your Grace in any way."

The Duke stiffened as if he had been impertinent, and Dubucheron feeling he had cast a fly over a fish which had not taken the bait, remained silent.

One of the cleverest things about him, considering he was a Frenchman, was that he knew when to talk and when to say nothing.

If a client did not respond immediately to a vague suggestion of what would interest him, he never pressed him but waited.

He had learnt from long experience, that sooner or later they were forced into declaring what they wanted, without his having to do anything about it.

As if the Duke had made up his mind not to continue the conversation, he said:

"I would like Miss Thoreau to see these pictures. As they are rightfully hers she may wish to keep them for herself, and frankly they are of no interest to me."

"I can understand that," Philippe Dubucheron said. "Shall I leave them with Your Grace and come back later?"

"No, no. I will ask her to see them now."

It had struck the Duke that he might learn a little more about these two people and their liaison if he saw them together.

Last night, he had been watching Una and not Dubucheron. Now he thought he would watch them both and doubtless he would find out something that he had not been aware of before.

He pulled upon the door and walked down the passage into the Hall.

"Go upstairs," he said to a footman, "and ask Mademoiselle Thoreau if she will join me in the Ante-chamber."

"M'mselle has left, Monsieur!"

"Left?"

The Duke frowned, then said:

"I mean the young lady who returned to the house with me just now."

"Yes, Monsieur. She left a few minutes later."

"But it is impossible! She went upstairs."

"Only half-way, Monsieur. Then she came down and asked Jacques to get her a *fiacre*."

"Which of you is Jacques?" the Duke enquired of the other footmen standing in the Hall.

One of the men stepped forward.

"I am Jacques, Monsieur."

"You called a *fiacre* for Mademoiselle?"

"Yes, Monsieur."

"Did she tell you where she wished to go?"

"Yes, Monsieur."

"What was the address?"

"9, Rue de l'Abreuville. It is in Montmartre."

The Duke was aware of this and he stood for a moment very still. Then he said sharply:

"Bring me my hat!"

It appeared as if by magic from a table beside the door.

He put it on his head and walked out into the courtyard.

His Chaise was waiting as he had ordered. He stepped into it, took the reins from the groom and as the man swung himself up behind, drove into the street.

He pushed his horses in a manner that would have surprised one of his own grooms in England. There had been no need for Dubucheron to tell him of the dangers that Una might encounter in Montmartre.

If Mr Beaumont had been aware that the *fin de siècle* had altered the attitudes and the behaviour of the French, the Duke was aware of it too.

He knew even better than his Comptroller, that beneath the bawdy gaiety of *La Belle Epoque,* there was vice and crime which had become uncontrollable.

It was not only the behaviour of the artists. There were anarchists who scorned Society's conventions and would deliberately behave like madmen.

There were not just a few eccentrics behaving in this manner, but a large number of men sympathetic to a political dogma which implied disastrous chaos and excessive individualism which was leading to suicide, both physical and mental.

To such people, a girl like Una would be an object of prey, with drink and drugs adding to their mental confusion.

There was also in France, and it was growing all the time into quite terrifying proportions, a great surge towards Black Magic, besides a busy white-slave traffic, which was always on the lookout for pretty young girls.

With regard to Black Magic, Paris had acquired a sinister reputation as being the centre for those who practised it.

Only the previous year, the Duke had read a book by a man called Huysmans who had suggested the existence of a widespread satanical cult in France and the dangers to young virgins who were an essential part of the sacrificial ritual.

The Duke had thought the book, which was called *La Bas* exaggerated when he read it, but now every aspect of the horrors that had been described, came back to him, as he connected them with Una.

He recalled all too vividly that Huysmans had said there were two main sects.

One was called the Palladists, worshipping Lucifer, the fallen angel of the true God; the other was called the Satanists who believed in the Christian divinity, but turned the Church ritual upside-down by transferring their allegiance to Satan.

The greatest danger of the Satanists was that they said a Mass over the naked body of a virgin on an altar which was surmounted by a Crucifix which was reversed.

As the stories of secret orgies in Masonic child-sacrifices and black masses seemed to gallop through the Duke's mind, he told himself that he was really being ridiculous.

It was very unlikely that in her father's Studio Una would come to any harm.

At the same time, there were other dangers from the current depravity of which he was quite certain she would be in total ignorance.

The Duke had also recently read a book by a Sociologist called Max Nordau which had not yet been published.

He had been shown the manuscript by a friend in England who was reading it to see if it contained any obvious errors, and the Duke had read it too.

With the title of *Degeneration*, he was quite certain that it would be a sensational best-seller and would convince many of its readers that civilisation was fast sinking into a mire of corruption.

The author described the symptoms of degeneration which he had observed during his years in Paris.

The book discussed the relations between the sexes and Nordau had written:

"Vice in Paris looks towards Sodom and Lesbos."

The Duke had always disliked anything that leaned towards perversion of any type, because he thought himself it harmed his own mind.

But now the words of Nordau's manuscript seemed to ring in his ears and to increase the fear within him that was almost like a live serpent, writhing in his body.

How could anyone like Una, if she was as innocent as she professed to be, have any knowledge of the snares, the horrors that were, if she was unprotected, lurking round every corner?

He could hardly believe it possible that she had, according to Dubucheron, gone alone to her father's Studio without a chaperon.

She might have been safe once — she undoubtedly had been — but to expect it a second time, was too much to ask, and the Duke drove his horses with a speed up the hill to Montmartre which left them sweating when he drew up in the Rue de l'Abreuville.

It was only as he stepped into the dingy hall and saw the dirty staircase ahead of him, that he told himself his fears were groundless.

He had not missed seeing the *fiacre* standing outside the building and he guessed it was the one in which Una had travelled from his house to Montmartre.

"I am making a fool of myself over a girl I had never seen until yesterday," the Duke said.

For the first time, he wondered what Dubucheron would think of his leaving the house without an explanation.

Because he felt he had been foolish in behaving in a manner that was very unlike his usual indifference to other people and their feelings, he walked up the staircase with a disdainful dignity.

As he did so, he decided that when he found Una, he would speak extremely sharply to her for abusing his hospitality by running off in such an absurd manner.

It was when he was half-way up the stairs that he heard her scream and he quickened his pace, to burst through the half-open door, as she screamed again and flung herself at him.

His arms went round her instinctively. Then he saw why she was screaming and the expression on the man's face, who was pursuing her.

"Take me . . . away! Take me . . . away!" Una gasped.

The Duke could feel her heart thumping against his and knew that her body was tense with fear.

He merely looked at the young painter and he too, was still.

The Duke had no need to speak. The expression in his eyes and on his face, would have cowed a far older man than the one facing him.

The artist capitulated.

"If that's your little *poule*," he said, half-aggressively, half in a conciliatory tone, "you should look after her better!"

"I agree with you," the Duke replied.

Turning, he pulled Una from the Studio and shut the door behind them. She was crying against his shoulder and his arm was still round her.

"It is all right," he said. "I will take you home. You should never have come here in the first place."

It was impossible for her to answer him and somehow with his arm round her, although the stairs were narrow, they managed to descend them side by side.

He helped her into the Chaise and paid the *fiacre*.

Only as the Duke drove off, did Una say in a voice that was broken with tears:

"I . . . I l-left my h-hat behind."

The Duke smiled.

"In which case you will undoubtedly have to go bareheaded, or let me buy you another one."

She did not answer but groped blindly in her hand-bag. The Duke, pulling a clean handkerchief from his breast pocket, gave it to her.

She took it from him and wiped her eyes.

"I . . . I am . . . s-sorry," she said in a very low voice, "b-but I did not . . . know there was . . . anyone there."

"Why did you go to the Studio?"

"I thought . . . perhaps there m-might be some . . . pictures of Papa's that I could s-sell and b-buy a . . . new gown . . . as you w-wanted me to."

Her voice was so incoherent that it was with difficulty that the Duke could hear what she was saying. Then he understood and after a moment, he said:

"You did not expect to find anyone else there?"

"N-no . . . that . . . artist only . . . moved in . . . this morning."

The Duke did not speak and after a moment Una went on:

"He-he wanted me to . . . pose for him . . . and I thought I might . . . do so as he would . . . p-pay . . . but I did not . . . understand that w-women posed in the . . . n-nude."

The Duke was surprised. Then he told himself that could not have been what she really thought.

"Your father was an artist," he said sharply. "He must have used models."

"O-only Mama," Una replied. "He . . . he never painted n-nudes."

The Duke thought it over. He supposed that if, in fact, Una had never been to an artist's Studio, she would not expect a model to sit in front of a man, with nothing on.

Then he asked:

"Why was that young swine chasing you?"

"When I s-said I would not . . . sit for him . . . he . . . he said he would . . . undress me!"

"Is that all he suggested?"

Una was silent and she put her handkerchief over her eyes, although the Duke did not think she was still crying.

He told himself angrily, that this should never have happened.

Then a mocking voice within him, asked if she could genuinely have been such a little fool as to get herself into such an impossible situation.

The fears he had entertained as he drove to Montmartre, were still in the back of his mind.

"Listen," he said, in a different tone of voice. "Listen to me, Una."

She raised her head and he thought because her eye-lashes were wet, that it made her look not only childlike, but also very pathetic.

"You will never," the Duke went on, "and this is an order — you will never again go about Paris alone! Do you understand?"

"I . . . I thought perhaps I should have . . . told you where I was going," Una said, "but if I had . . . found some of Papa's pictures I could have . . . bought a new gown. I . . . wanted it to be a s-surprise."

"So that was why you went to Montmartre!"

"I did so want you to think I looked . . . attractive."

"You ridiculous child! Of course you look attractive! You must know you are extremely pretty, far prettier than anyone I have seen for a long time."

'Or ever!' the Duke thought, but he had no intention of saying too much or committing himself.

He was well aware that Una was looking at him with wide eyes, a radiant expression on her face, that he had never seen before.

"Do you . . . mean that?" she asked. "Do you really and truly think I am pretty?"

"Really and truly!" the Duke answered, "and as an artist's daughter, you will understand that because I think you are pretty, I want to give you a frame that is worthy of your looks."

"I thought it would be . . . impossible for you to . . . admire me, after seeing so many lovely women in the Restaurant at luncheon today, and how . . . attractive Mademoiselle

Yvette Joyant . . . looked last night."

"I think it was your father who said that just as there were different sorts of pictures, there are different sorts of women. Men, fortunately, have different tastes."

Una clasped her hands together, the Duke's handkerchief in the centre of them. Then she asked a little shyly:

"I . . . if I . . . dine with you tonight in the only . . . gown I have . . . you will not . . . be ashamed of me?"

"It was unkind of me to have said that," the Duke confessed, "and quite frankly, I said it to make it easier for you to accept the gowns I wanted to give you."

"You . . . you said I could . . . think about it."

"If what you have just done was the result, then I would rather you stopped thinking and left it to me."

"Th-that is . . . what I would . . . like to do," she answered, "but . . ."

"Are you telling me there are still 'buts'?" the Duke queried.

"I would . . . like to sort it out in my . . . mind," she said, "and have time to pray for an . . . answer."

"Is that what you usually do?" the Duke asked curiously.

Una nodded.

"If I pray very . . . very hard about . . . something, then I am usually told what to do."

"Well, I hope whoever is listening to you in Heaven, will realise that unlike the lilies of the field, you need something a little more substantial to cover you, than the beauty of your skin."

The Duke spoke dryly, but he saw the colour creep into Una's face.

After a moment she said:

"Perhaps if you gave me just . . . one gown that was not . . . too expensive . . . Mama would not be . . . angry with me."

"I suppose the choice is," the Duke said, "whether your mother, who is not with us, will be angry, or whether I, who am, will be. It will be entirely up to you who you placate."

She turned towards him impulsively, her face lifted to his and she said:

"Please . . . I could not bear you to be . . . cross with me, after having been so . . . kind . . . and it would be . . . thrilling . . . really thrilling to have a new gown."

The Duke had a sudden feeling of triumph. He was the victor in what had been an unusual and quite strenuous contest.

Then as he glanced down into Una's upraised eyes and saw the expression in them, he thought perhaps, after all, it was a hollow victory.

6

The Duke drove into the courtyard with a flourish and Una got out, feeling that the servants were staring at her tear-stained eyes and noticing that she had lost her hat.

The Duke took her arm and drew her into the Salon. As the door closed behind them, he said:

"I am going to give you a glass of champagne. I feel you need it after what you have been through."

"I . . . I am . . . sorry," Una faltered.

"It is not your fault," he replied. "Someone should have warned you that it would be crazy to go about Paris alone."

He moved towards the grog-tray as he spoke and heard Una say just below her breath:

"I am . . . alone."

He poured some champagne into two glasses and carried them back to her, where she stood on the hearth-rug.

He thought as he did so, that she looked very lovely despite the woe-begone expression on her little face and the tear-stains on her cheeks.

He knew that any other woman of his acquaintance would have, at this moment, been repairing her looks in the mirror.

Una took the glass from him and asked as she did so:

"Are you . . . angry with . . . me?"

"No, of course not," the Duke answered, "but you might remember in future, that it would be wise to tell me what you intend to do, before you do it."

"But you . . . may not be . . . there."

"That is something I want to talk to you about," the Duke answered, "but not at this moment. We have the whole evening in front of us."

She looked up at him and her eyes lightened.

"You will still take me . . . out to . . . dinner?"

"I should be very disappointed if I had to dine alone," he replied.

Her eyes met his and something she did not quite understand made her heart start beating excitedly and she found it hard to look away from him.

The Duke was silent for a moment as if he was considering something. Then he said:

"I have a picture to show you which I

think you would like to see again. Wait here!"

He left the Salon and went into the Ante-chamber which he found was empty but Julius Thoreau's canvasses were still propped up on the sofa.

As he picked up the one he wanted, the Clerk-of-the-Chambers said from the door:

"The gentleman left, Your Grace. He said he would call again whenever it was convenient."

The Duke nodded his acknowledgement of the message and went back into the Salon.

Una looked up at him enquiringly, and as he held the canvas so that she could see it, she gave a cry.

"You have it! You have Papa's picture of me! That is what I hoped I should find when I went to his Studio."

"If you had asked me, I could have told you it was here waiting for you," the Duke replied, but he was smiling and his words were not a rebuke.

Una, holding the picture in both hands, took it to the window.

"I was nine when Papa painted this," she said, "but he would never finish it."

"Why not?" the Duke enquired.

"He said it was too conventional, too ordinary, and also I was a bad . . . model. I would not stand still."

She glanced at the Duke as she spoke and he laughed, as if they shared a private joke.

But he knew that she would not wish to refer to what had just happened with the artist who had wished to undress her.

"That was your home?" he asked, pointing to the house in the background.

"It was much prettier than that," Una answered. "Papa has not painted the wistaria which climbed up one wall or the roses which scented every room."

Her voice was soft as she reminisced and the Duke said:

"You were happy there?"

"Very happy. Mama made everything such fun, even though I suppose we were very poor."

There was a little pause. Then Una said again almost beneath her breath:

"But not as . . . poor as I am now."

The Duke put his hand on her shoulder.

"Una . . ." he began.

At that moment the door opened and a voice announced:

"M'Lord Stanton, Your Grace!"

The Duke turned round in surprise and so did Una.

A middle-aged, red-faced man with a

dark moustache was coming into the room.

"Hello Blaze!" he exclaimed. "I am surprised to see you. I had no idea you were in Paris."

Reluctantly the Duke walked towards the new-comer, to shake his hand.

"I arrived yesterday," he explained, speaking in what those who knew him would have called his 'cold voice'.

"Well, it is a blessing you are here," Lord Stanton said, "because you can put me up for the night. I have just missed the Sleeper Train to Nice by five minutes!"

The Duke did not reply and he went on:

"I am off to stay with Gertie, but there was a breakdown just before the train from Calais got into Paris. So I am stranded, which is extremely annoying."

"I am sure it is," the Duke agreed.

"I thought your house might be open and I could stay here. Anyway, when I arrived I was told you were in residence. That was a bit of luck, I thought!"

Lord Stanton laughed heartily, as if he had made a joke.

Then his eyes were on Una.

She was looking very lovely with the sunshine behind her, haloing her hair in gold.

Her figure, with its tiny waist, silhouetted against the window, was an enticement of which she was completely unaware.

It was obvious Lord Stanton was waiting and the Duke said:

"Una, let me introduce my cousin, Lord Stanton — Miss Una Thoreau!"

Lord Stanton moved towards her with the obvious eagerness of a middle-aged man who sees a very pretty girl.

"I am delighted to meet you," he said. "But I might have expected it! Blaze always has the prettiest women around him!"

Una looked a little shy at the compliment, and the Duke said:

"Miss Thoreau and I were just admiring her picture painted by her father."

"Let me see it," Lord Stanton suggested. Peering over Una's shoulder he exclaimed:

"Is that you? Well, you have grown quite a lot since that was done, and very much prettier too!"

Again he laughed and Una looked a little uncomfortably at the Duke.

"I expect you would like to go and change," he said. "We will leave here at about eight o'clock."

"That will be . . . lovely."

She put the picture down on a chair, gave Lord Stanton a polite little smile and walked towards the door.

He watched her go, then when they were

alone, said to the Duke:

"By jove, Blaze, you can certainly choose them! Prettiest little filly I have seen in a long time. And English! I should have thought when you came to Paris, you would prefer the French breed."

The Duke stiffened.

"It is nothing like that, Bertie," he said. "Miss Thoreau is staying here as my guest, and I am an admirer of her father's pictures."

"And of his daughter, eh?" Lord Stanton said, nudging him with his arm. "Well, I don't blame you! She is certainly a very different type from Rose."

"I have already told you," the Duke replied, in a colder voice, "that what you are insinuating, may I say in an extremely vulgar manner, is not true. Miss Thoreau is very young and as you well know, I am not interested in young girls."

As he finished speaking he rang the bell.

"I will arrange for a room to be ready for you. Do you wish to dine here?"

"Good God, no! I am not dining alone in Paris," Lord Stanton replied. "I shall look in at 'The Travellers' and find a friend or two who will take me on the town."

"I hope you enjoy yourself," the Duke said frigidly, as a servant came into the room for his instructions.

Having arranged for his cousin's comfort, the Duke went to find Mr Beaumont in his office.

His Comptroller rose from his desk.

"I did not know Your Grace was back."

"I am not only back," the Duke replied, "but Bertie Stanton has arrived here demanding that he stay the night!"

"Lord Stanton!" Mr Beaumont exclaimed.

"I thought I gave you explicit instructions that I was not to be disturbed by visitors," the Duke said angrily.

He saw the look of consternation on his Comptroller's face and added:

"I do not suppose it was your fault, or that of the servants. I know what Bertie is like: he would push his way into Buckingham Palace if it suited him!"

"I can only apologise," Mr Beaumont said.

"It is a damned nuisance," the Duke commented. "But he is leaving for Nice in the morning and you might see that he is on the early train."

"I certainly will!" Mr Beaumont said in a penitent tone.

Then as the Duke would have left him, he said:

"There is a letter here which had just arrived from the British Embassy. It came in the Diplomatic Bag."

He held it out to the Duke who looked at it, he thought, somewhat apprehensively, and then opened the heavily crested envelope.

He read slowly what was contained in the letter while Mr Beaumont waited.

After quite a considerable pause the Duke said:

"Do you know what is in this letter?"

"How could I?" Mr Beaumont enquired.

"It is from the Prime Minister. He informs me in confidence, that the Queen has asked him to go to Windsor in three days' time to discuss the appointment of a new Viceroy in Ireland. He is anxious to put forward my name."

"I can only congratulate Your Grace most wholeheartedly!" Mr Beaumont said.

"I have not said I am going to accept," the Duke protested.

"It is a job you could do most admirably. If you remember, I told you when you were standing at the crossroads."

The Duke looked at the letter again and re-read one paragraph which he had not mentioned to Mr Beaumont:

It said:

"Her majesty is likely to raise the point that it is usual and advisable that the Viceroy should be married, but that, I imagine, is a problem which could be quite easily solved in the near future."

The Duke knew that the Prime Minister was referring to the fact that everyone in London Society had been, for some time, expecting him to announce his engagement to Rose Caversham.

That he had no intention of marrying her would be, of course, an excellent excuse for refusing the appointment.

At the same time, he could not help thinking that the Prime Minister would wish him to accept it.

He knew that his recent speeches in the House of Lords, his very generous support of the Party, and the fact that the Prime Minister had often consulted him on various matters, accounted for it.

He suddenly thought that if he did refuse, he would feel in a way, that he had betrayed a friendship which he valued and respected.

He realised Mr Beaumont was waiting for him to speak.

"I shall think it over," he said, putting the letter in his pocket. "It is too serious a decision to make quickly."

"Naturally, Your Grace," Mr Beaumont agreed. "At the same time, I think that as the position you will hold in Ireland will be a difficult one, it is in fact, a challenge which you would enjoy."

'Another challenge!' the Duke thought to himself, as he went up the stairs towards his bedroom. 'There seems to be no end to them!'

Seated in the Restaurant to which the Duke had taken Una for dinner, she thought that the most exciting thing that had ever happened to her was that she was dining alone with the Duke.

When she had been changing for dinner, she had, at first, felt apprehensive about her gown, hoping that he would take her somewhere very quiet so that she would not be conspicuous.

Secondly, she had been afraid that they would not dine alone and there would be a party, as there had been last night.

She felt that the Duke might be obliged to ask his cousin, the red-faced Lord Stanton, to dine with them, and she felt that would spoil everything.

It had been so wonderful to talk to the Duke alone at luncheon and to drive with him in the Park.

She knew that, when he had appeared in the Studio just when she had needed him most, he had been like a Knight in armour coming to save her from a very fierce and very frightening dragon.

"He is so wonderful!" she said to herself.

She wanted to talk to him, she wanted to be with him, with no-one else to intrude on their conversation.

"Oh, please God, let Lord Stanton dine somewhere else," she found herself praying.

Then she was instantly ashamed that she should pray for anything so trivial and so selfish.

When she went downstairs to the Salon, she had found the Duke magnificent in his evening-clothes and alone.

She did not realise that her whole face lit up with delight because her fears were unfounded and as she moved towards the Duke, she saw that he was smiling.

At the same time, there was that expression in his eyes that had made her heart beat so quickly when they had been looking at the picture together.

When Una was dressing, the maid had offered to arrange her hair and she had accepted gratefully.

While she had been sitting in front of the dressing-table there had been a knock at the door and the maid had come back with a spray of small white orchids in her hand.

"A corsage, M'mselle," she smiled.

Una gave a little cry of delight.

"It is exactly what I want!"

She took it from the maid, asking: "Shall I wear it in the front of my gown or at the shoulder?"

"Why not in your hair, M'mselle?"

"What a good idea!" Una exclaimed, "and it will make me look *chic* and I hope, a little more sophisticated."

In actual fact, the orchids in her hair merely made her look like the goddess of spring.

The Duke thought that all the tiaras in the Wolstanton collection could not have been more becoming.

When she reached his side Una said:

"Thank you for the lovely orchids. Will you please look at them and not at my gown, which you do not like?"

"I shall find it difficult to look at anything but your face," the Duke answered.

Una was surprised, and when her eyes met his, she blushed.

"The carriage is waiting," he said, "and I am going to take you to somewhere quiet, not, may I say, because I am ashamed of your appearance, but because I want to talk to you."

"That is the nicest thing you could say to me!" Una cried.

When they arrived at the *Grand Vefour* she thought, in fact, it was just the sort of place she would rather be in with the Duke, than somewhere big and noisy with a Band which might prevent her hearing all he was saying to her.

The *Grand Vefour* was, the Duke told Una, exactly the same as it had been when it was first opened at the time of the Revolution.

The painted panels on the walls, huge mirrors, the comfortable red plush sofas had served generations of distinguished patrons who appreciated good food.

Una looked round her with delight as the Duke took a long time in choosing their meal.

Then at last, he turned to her with a smile to say:

"Now we have nothing to do but enjoy ourselves."

"That is what I am doing already," Una replied. "It is very exciting to be here with you . . . alone."

"I had no intention of having a party," the Duke answered. "If you want to go somewhere amusing afterwards, we have a great number of places to choose from."

"I just want to be with you."

She spoke with a deep note of sincerity in her voice.

It made the Duke wonder to himself if she meant it in the way he would wish her to, or if it was just an automatic expression of the childish pleasure she was showing in the whole evening.

When he was dressing for dinner, he had known that the suspicions he had felt about her had almost been extinguished.

She was Julius Thoreau's daughter. There was no doubt about that.

And he was beginning to believe, although there was just a lingering doubt in his mind, that she had really met Dubucheron for the first time yesterday when she had arrived from Florence.

If that was so, then her purity and innocence owed nothing to acting.

"I will talk to her tonight," the Duke said to himself, "and then I shall know whether it is necessary for me to go on being suspicious."

If that was so, a whole number of problems presented themselves.

He had meant, of course, when he had carried Una off from the Moulin Rouge, to make love to her and enjoy his time in Paris with a beautiful woman as he had done on

230

so many other occasions.

Everything had actually been made very easy for him, because her trunk was at his house, and when he had ordered it to be taken upstairs to the *Chambre des Roses*, she would sleep in the room which communicated with his own.

It was only because they were both tired last night that he had not opened the door, as he had intended.

But tonight there was no such restriction and he was quite certain that by the end of the evening Una would express her willingness for him to be her lover.

And yet a question still remained in his mind.

Had the elusive manner in which she had brushed aside or prevented any show of intimacy between them during the day, been intentional?

Or was it merely because she was so innocent she did not understand in any way, what was expected of her?

There was also the problem, the Duke thought, that if she was really alone, as she said she would be when he returned to England, would he feel justified in leaving her at the mercy of the only so-called "friend" she had, in Philippe Dubucheron?

He was well aware what use Dubucheron

would make of her, and everything in him revolted at the idea of her being exploited as he was trying to exploit her now.

Sitting beside her in the *Grand Vefour* the Duke wondered if any other woman could look so pure, so untouched and at the same time, exude an enchanting fascination that he was beginning to find irresistible.

They talked about trivial things while they ate the delicious dishes which the Duke had ordered. Una found she was quite hungry and ready to do justice to everything that was put in front of her.

Finally, when the coffee came and the Duke sat back with a glass of brandy, he said:

"Now! We can talk about ourselves and that means principally about you!"

"I have . . . so little to tell," Una said, "and you have so . . . much."

She paused, then she added:

"I felt somehow just now, although it may seem foolish, that you were thinking about something different; something more important than your dinner."

"That sounds as if I was being discourteous."

"No, of course not, you were being more interesting than anyone I have ever met," Una said.

"Then what are you saying to me?"

"It is just something I saw before in what you called my 'magic mirror'; something that happened, or was going to happen and you were thinking about it."

The Duke was astounded.

"How could you know that?" he asked.

"I do not . . . know," Una said truthfully. "I just thought it, and that meant I felt it."

"You are a very astonishing person."

He was silent for a moment, then he said:

"I think it only fair to tell you that you are quite right and what you anticipated has happened."

"It has?" Una asked.

"I received a letter today," the Duke said, "from the Prime Minister."

"Of England?"

"Yes, the Marquess of Salisbury."

Una waited, her eyes on his face, and the Duke went on:

"He suggested that I should become the next Viceroy of Ireland!"

"Viceroy?" Una repeated in an awed tone.

"It is of course, a great compliment, that he should consider me," the Duke went on, "especially as I am not as old as the usual run of Viceroys."

"And you will be going to Ireland at once?"

"I have not yet accepted the appointment," the Duke said, "but I imagine that as the last Viceroy is retiring, the Queen will not wish to wait very long before appointing another."

"I am sure you are exactly the right person for such a position," Una said.

"Why do you say that?" the Duke asked.

"I have read about Ireland, their troubles and their difficulties," Una explained, "and I think if anyone could help them, it would be you."

The Duke looked at her in surprise.

He had not expected her to know anything about the Irish problem. Then he said:

"Of course, you realise if I decide to go to Ireland, it means that we should have to say goodbye to each other. I can hardly arrive in Dublin with a very beautiful young Curator."

"No . . . of course . . . not."

"And yet you still urge me to accept the position?" the Duke asked.

Una looked away from him and he thought it was because she did not wish him to see the expression in her eyes.

"If you are right . . . the right person for Ireland," she said, "which I am . . . sure you are . . . then it is your duty to . . . accept the

Prime Minister's suggestion."

"You are thinking of me?"

"But of course!"

"And what do you imagine you will do?"

"I will find . . . somewhere to . . . go," Una replied, "but I do not want to live alone in Paris."

"Whether you want it or not," the Duke said harshly, "it is something that must not happen. I will make arrangements for you, perhaps to come to England."

As he spoke, he wondered what arrangements he could make and if Una was alone in London would things be any better?

'She is too lovely,' he thought, 'and far too young to look after herself."

As if Una sensed that he was worrying about her, she said quickly:

"Please . . . you must not think about me. You have only just met me . . . and you have already been so kind and so understanding."

She drew in her breath and went on:

"When you leave Paris, I will ask Monsieur Dubucheron to find me a quiet pension or lodgings where I can stay until I can find . . . some work."

When she mentioned Dubucheron who was obviously the only person to whom she could turn, the Duke felt that if he left her in such hands, he would be committing a crime.

He told himself that he had never felt like this about any woman before and had always been certain, once he had finished with them, that their future plans did not concern him in any way.

But Una was different. She was so young, so helpless and so incredibly lovely.

The Duke had not missed the looks that Una had received from other men in the Restaurant, and he noticed one old man who was sitting opposite them had never taken his eyes from her face, ever since they arrived.

Without choosing his words he said, almost savagely:

"The best thing I can do is to forget Ireland, and look after you. God knows, you need someone to take care of you!"

The tone of his voice made Una look at him in sheer astonishment. Then she said:

"But of course you must not . . . think of . . . anything like . . . that. How can I matter or be of any . . . importance beside being . . . Viceroy of Ireland?"

Then as if she felt she had taken him too seriously, she said:

"If I am being a . . . nuisance, then I will . . . leave tomorrow. Mama used to say there is nothing more tiresome than a visitor who will not leave when they have outstayed their welcome."

"Do you think that applies to you?" the Duke asked.

Again she found it difficult to look at him and she made a nervous little gesture with her hands before she replied:

"You said Mama would not approve of my staying with you without a chaperon, and I thought tonight that your cousin . . . Lord Stanton . . . thought so . . . too."

"Nothing we do or do not do need concern Cousin Bertie," the Duke said angrily. "I told Beaumont that I would not be disturbed by any visitors, but he forced his way in. He always has been a pushing creature with whom I have nothing in common."

"But he is your cousin."

"Exactly!" the Duke replied, "and that is why once he was in the house I could hardly turn him out and tell him to find somewhere else to stay. But he will leave tomorrow, and then we can forget about him."

Una felt a gladness that she could not describe sweep over her.

The Duke wanted to be alone with her, as she wanted to be alone with him. It was so wonderful and there were no words in which she could express it.

Then because she thought it was selfish of her, she said:

"At the same time Lord Stanton is your . . . relative and relatives have . . . special privileges."

"The trouble with my relatives is that I have too many of them," the Duke said.

"You are lucky," Una replied. "I have none."

"How can anybody have none?"

It flashed through his mind that once again she was playing the poor little orphan girl with nowhere to go and rather overdoing the role.

"But it is true in effect," Una said. "Papa lost all touch with his family when he left England, and Mama's relations were so angry because she ran away with him that they never spoke to her again."

"So you really are alone," the Duke remarked, "except that I am here."

"You know how . . . thankful I am for that," Una said. "If you had not . . . saved me this afternoon, I . . ."

"Forget this afternoon," the Duke said quickly. "Let us just remember that we are here together. We are in Paris, the city of gaiety and laughter."

"And a city of a great number of other things," he told himself, but that was not something he wished to discuss with Una.

"Do you know what I would like to do now?" Una asked.

"What?"

"I would like to see Paris at night."

She saw an expression on the Duke's face and added:

"No, not the . . . places of . . . entertainment like the Moulin Rouge. I did not . . . mean that."

"Then what did you mean?" the Duke asked.

"Perhaps it would bore you," Una said humbly, "but I thought if we could drive along the banks of the Seine and see the Place de la Concorde when it is lit up and the Champs Élysées, it would be a very . . . exciting thing to do."

Her eyes searched his face to see his reaction and when he smiled, she said:

"You are quite sure it would not . . . bore you?"

"I can imagine nothing I would rather do," the Duke replied, "and fortunately we can order the hood of the carriage in which we came here, to be opened."

Una clasped her hands together.

"I wonder," the Duke said reflectively, "if, in a few years, the idea of seeing Paris by night will seem so entertaining."

"You mean that when I am older, I shall . . . want to do . . . other things?"

"That is what I was saying."

"Does one ever get too old to enjoy the beauty of things that are natural rather than artificial?"

"For some people it is inevitable."

"Then I hope I am not like that," Una said. "I thought when I left Florence, it would be very exciting to see Paris, but last night when we were at the Moulin Rouge, I realised that it was not like . . . anything I had expected and in fact, I thought it was . . . ugly and rather . . . frightening."

"The Moulin Rouge was certainly not for you, the right introduction to Paris. There are other places that are quite different, and of course, at your age you should be going to Balls and parties."

"I would much rather be . . . talking to you."

"Which, if you were a Society Débutante, you would not be allowed to do," the Duke smiled.

"Why not?"

"Because well-brought-up young ladies are kept away from men until they are married."

"And if they are not allowed to be with men, how do they get married?" Una enquired practically.

"Marriages in England, as in France, as you must know, are arranged."

"The girls used to talk about that at the Convent," Una said, "and I always thought it was horrible, unnatural! How could one marry a man one did not love . . . someone one hardly . . . knew?"

She gave a little shudder.

"I would be frightened," she said, "unless I loved someone as Mama loved Papa."

The Duke thought that marriage was not a subject that he wished to discuss with Una.

Without replying to her last remark, he called for his bill and paid it with what Una thought uneasily was an enormous amount of money.

Then she told herself that to refer to it would be ill-bred and she resisted an impulse to tell him that she felt embarrassed at having cost him so much.

After all, if he was not dining with her, he would have been dining with somebody else.

At the same time, she felt a little uncomfortable.

She was beginning to think that despite the fact that the Duke had said he wanted no visitors in his house, Monsieur Dubucheron had deliberately forced her upon him.

The mere fact of leaving her trunk at the house when they went to the Moulin Rouge, was more than a broad hint that she had nowhere to go.

"It is too late now," she told herself, "but I should have insisted on Monsieur Dubucheron telling me what he had planned for me before we went to the Duke's house for dinner."

She knew she had been swept along as if on a wave from the moment Monsieur Dubucheron had returned to the Studio to tell her he had sold her father's picture.

It struck her as she stepped into the carriage which was waiting outside, that once the Duke had returned to England to take up his appointment as Viceroy of Ireland, she would be alone, and it would be very . . . very . . . frightening.

The hood had been opened and the footman put a fur rug over their knees. When the man had climbed up on the box, the Duke took Una's hand in his.

She had not expected him to do so and he felt her finger stiffen as if in surprise, then tremble in his.

It gave him the feeling that he held a small song-bird or a butterfly in his grasp and he wondered why a young woman he had never known before had such an effect on him.

He had certainly never treated any woman he desired so gently or exercised such control over his feelings, and no woman whom he had been with alone as he was with Una, had ever been so elusive.

Una used no feminine wiles upon him and made no obvious effort to attract him physically.

At the same time, the Duke was experienced enough to realise that the way she looked at him was not only trusting, but showed an unconcealed admiration.

He found himself wondering what else she felt and he puzzled as to what her real feelings could be.

With any other woman he would have known that, if she was not in love with him in the fullest sense of the word, she was certainly physically attracted. He would have seen the flicker of fire in her eyes even before there was any glow in his.

It suddenly struck him that the most intriguing and fascinating thing he could imagine, would be to awaken Una to love.

The little tremor of her fingers was, he knew, not that of fear, but of excitement. He was sure that if he held her body close against his, the same little tremors would run through it as she awoke to the first stirrings of desire.

He found his heart was beating fast and there was a sudden throbbing in his temples that made him want to pull Una into his arms and kiss her.

It was, he acknowledged, what he had wished to do ever since he met her.

He had in fact, restrained himself simply because he was afraid of frightening her.

Now he thought he would deny his own manhood if he did not speak to her of the feelings within him.

They had reached the Place de la Concorde, where the golden globes on the beautifully ornamented lamps revealed the fountains throwing their water iridescent like a thousand rainbows up towards the stars.

Una's fingers tightened on his.

"It is so lovely!"

"And so are you!" the Duke replied. "Tell me, Una, what do you feel, not about Paris, but about me?"

She looked round at him and he released her hand and put his arm round her shoulders to draw her close.

He knew he had surprised her and after a moment she said in a tremulous little voice:

"I . . . thought today you were like a . . . Knight in armour . . . coming to . . . save me."

"That is what I want to be," the Duke said, "but I think the damsels in distress who were rescued by the Knights who saved them from the dragon or some other loathsome monsters would have welcomed any man whatever he looked like."

"You . . . know how . . . grateful I am."

"Gratitude is something you can give anybody. Look in your magic mirror and tell me what you feel about me."

"You know I think you are the most . . . magnificent man I have ever seen," Una said, "and you are very . . . clever . . . and very kind . . . and . . ."

She paused.

"And?" the Duke prompted.

"And just the right person to be the . . . Viceroy of Ireland!"

"I told you that I thought I should stay and look after you," the Duke said.

"You were only joking when you said that," Una answered. "I shall be . . . all right."

"How could I be sure of that?" the Duke enquired.

"I could . . . write to you. It would make it . . . easier than to . . . lose you."

"You are quite content to lose me?"

"Not . . . content," Una said. "It will be . . . horrible when you have . . . gone . . . but I shall have all the . . . things we have . . .

done together and . . . everything you have . . . said to me . . . to remember."

"I can think of better things than what has happened so far," the Duke said.

He wanted to kiss Una, but he felt it was not something he could do in an open carriage with the backs of the coachman and the footman sitting beside him towering above them.

Instead, he tightened his arm about her, as he said:

"Come as close to me as you can. I want you against me."

Una turned her head to lay it against his shoulder.

"You make me feel so . . . safe," she murmured. "I suppose . . . really . . . I am frightened of being . . . alone . . . I keep telling myself I have to . . . cope . . . I have to look after myself . . . it is just that . . . I do not know . . . where to begin."

It flashed through the Duke's mind that he would take her to England with him and set her up in a house with every comfort where she would be safe until he could spend his holidays with her.

Perhaps later, his thoughts went on, he would be able to take her to Ireland. He would find some excuse for having her near him.

Then he told himself that even if she agreed to live with him, under such conditions, it would be certain sooner or later, to cause a scandal.

The Press ferreted out everything and that would not only injure Una but damage his own reputation and that of the British Crown which had appointed him.

"What the devil am I to do?" the Duke asked himself.

He felt that whatever happened, whatever the penalties, he could not give Una up.

The mere fact of touching her had made his blood seem as if it was on fire and he knew that his desire for her was increasing every moment and every second they were together.

"I want you!" he wanted to cry aloud. "I want you unbearably!"

But he knew if he said anything so unrestrained, she would shrink away from him nervously and perhaps try wildly to escape, as she had tried to escape the young painter this afternoon.

The Duke suddenly had an awful feeling that the sands were running out, time was going too quickly.

He knew that he wanted to woo Una very gently, to feel her respond to him, as a flower will open its petals to the sunshine.

This was not a fiery, impulsive, unrestrained urge in the mere physical sense. This, he told himself, was far more subtle, far more alluring.

The Duke had always looked on love as a romantic name for what was a physical union between two people who attracted each other chemically.

He had never indulged in the poetical fantasies of some of his contemporaries, and as he had grown older, he had been quite coldly analytical about what he felt for the women to whom he made love.

He found himself, however much they aroused him, critical of their faults, their flaws and their little habits which even at the very onset of an affair, he would find irritating.

It was extraordinary, but in the time he had been with Una she had never shown him any side of her nature that he had not found delightful. He had never found anything she said stupid or out of place.

The grace of her body and the beauty of her face had, he thought, something spiritual about them which he had never found in any other woman.

But because she held him at bay not by anything she said or did, but simply because of some aura of purity that encircled her, he knew as he controlled his desire to make passionate love to her, that he could not lose her.

"Damn Ireland!" he said in his heart. "I have found something far more important to me personally."

Because he was thinking so deeply they drove in silence until Una gave a little exclamation of delight and raised her head from his shoulder.

He saw that she was looking at the Seine, silver beneath the starlight, with its bridges spanning it like jewelled bangles.

Una moved from the shelter of his arms to sit upright so that she could see more.

The Duke watched her profile and knew that she attracted him to such an extent that he had precipitately and astonishingly fallen in love.

He could never remember in the whole of his long and varied career with women, feeling as he did now.

Like a diver who had sought for years at the bottom of the sea for a perfect pearl, he felt an elation which made him step out of his ordinary self and gasp at the wonder of it.

"This is the real Paris," Una murmured. "What we saw last night was only the imitation."

It was typical of her, the Duke thought, to say exactly the right thing. He drew her back against him and wrapped the rug over her, thinking she had already given him a happiness that he had never known before.

They drove for a long time and it was if there was no need for them to talk to each other; their hearts and their souls were speaking without words.

Only as they reached the Faubourg St Honoré did Una move and the Duke took his arm from her.

In the lights shining over the entrance, he could see the expression in her eyes and thought it was that of a child who had been in Wonderland.

They stepped out, passed through the Hall and into the Salon as if they both knew what the other was wanting.

The lights were low and shaded and the beautiful room seemed exactly the background, the Duke thought, he would have chosen for Una.

The door closed behind them.

She stood for a moment, looking at him, then he was not certain whether she moved or he did, but she was in his arms and her face was turned up to his.

"My darling, my lovely one!" the Duke said and his lips came down on hers.

He felt the softness and the innocence of her lips and he kissed her very gently, almost as if he was touching a flower.

He felt, as he had anticipated, that her body quivered against his and he knew she was, in fact, the butterfly he had captured and that if he was not gentle, he could destroy it.

His kiss became a little more insistent, but still he kept himself under control and he knew that there was something spiritual and perfect in their kiss which was passionate and yet in a way, sacred.

He raised his head, and Una said, her voice a little breathless and unsteady:

"Th-that was . . . a perfect end to a most . . . perfect and . . . wonderful . . . night!"

Her voice seemed almost to break on the last words. Then to the Duke's astonishment, before he could hardly realise what was happening, she had moved across the room and he was alone.

He stood for a moment throbbing with the ecstasy she had aroused in him and with her voice singing in his ears.

Then he told himself it was what he might have expected, but what she would not understand was that he wanted her to stay.

He wanted to make love to her and eventually make her his, completely and absolutely.

"She is so young," he told himself. "I must be gentle. I must do nothing too quickly."

He walked across the room and poured himself out a drink, then pulled back one of the curtains to stand at the window looking out over the garden.

Beyond the trees there was the glow of lights from the Champs Élysées blending with the glittering stars overhead.

"I am in love!" the Duke told himself. "In love, as I never believed it possible to be."

But he asked himself what he could do about it.

He knew now, that he wanted Una, not only as his mistress but with him for ever. Then he laughed at the absurdity of such an idea.

As the Duke of Wolstanton, he belonged to an ancient family, second in importance only to the Royal Family.

How could he possibly take as his wife the daughter of an artist?

It would defame the family name. It would bring disgrace to the Stantons, who had played their part in the history of England and who, good or bad in their private lives, had always been dignified and proud in public.

"It is impossible!" the Duke said aloud.

Yet he knew that with every breath he drew, he wanted Una more.

He tried to tell himself that once she was his, in the physical sense of the word, everything would be all right.

They would have a happy time together and when he left her, he would see that she had plenty of money for the rest of her life.

But he knew that was not what he wanted. He wanted something quite different: something which could never be assuaged by the mere physical contact of two bodies.

He was in love and love was exactly what the poets had written about it, the artists painted and the musicians composed.

It seemed incredible that he had had to wait until he was nearly thirty-five to feel like this, and then to fall in love overnight, when he was looking for just a week or two's fun in the most frivolous city in the world.

"What am I to do? God in Heaven, what am I to do?" the Duke asked aloud.

He felt as if his own question echoed and re-echoed back at him, but there was no reply.

Two hours later the Duke walked upstairs to his bedroom.

When he entered it, he found his tired

Valet waiting up for him, and when he was undressed and the man had left him, he did not get into bed, but stood at the window thinking.

The communicating door into Una's room was only a few feet away from him, and yet he knew he would not open it.

In the past two hours, while he had been thinking about her, he had known one thing irrefutably: that he could not seduce her and leave her.

His love was too great for that. He wanted her, God knows, he wanted her and his whole being cried out for the softness and sweetness of her.

But because he loved her, he would not spoil anything so perfect and so utterly and completely beautiful.

"Tomorrow I will find a solution as to what I can do for her," he told himself, "but I must not touch her again. If I do, nothing will stop me from loving her and making her mine!"

Everything that was best in the Duke and which had been overlaid by years of indolence and pleasure-seeking, was swept away by a love that was greater than desire — finer and more glorious than any physical need.

Because he loved her, he wanted to lay at

Una's feet everything that was perfect and beautiful to match what she personified in herself.

Nothing harsh, ugly or cruel should touch her, and that included his own need for her.

But what he thought and what he felt were two different things. In his mind his love was sanctified, but his body craved for her agonisingly.

It struck him suddenly that this was his Gethsemane, which comes to every man, sooner or later in his life, a time of crisis which he must accept.

"I thought love meant happiness," he said, "but this is agony, torture, crucifixion!"

It was then as the words seemed to go out into the darkness of the night, that he heard the door behind him being pushed open.

7

Una had left the Salon in an indescribable rapture.

As she reached the sanctuary of her bedroom, she thought that whatever happened in the future, she would have something to remember, something so precious, so perfect that she knew she would never experience anything like it again, however long she lived.

She knew now, that what she had felt for the Duke ever since she had first seen him, was love.

Only because she was so ignorant of men and even of herself, she had not realised that what she felt and what occurred when they looked into each other's eyes was the love she had always believed she would find, at some time in her life.

It had come to her with a glory and a radiance that was Divine.

She had wanted to remain in the Duke's arms, for him to go on kissing her, but because she was so unusually perceptive where he was concerned, she thought it might make it difficult for him to leave her.

She realised that he must do his duty and accept the position of Viceroy of Ireland.

She was not so foolish as to think it was possible for him to hold such an important post and at the same time, for them to remain as they were now.

To be with him was like being in Heaven, but she knew it was unconventional and wrong for her to stay alone, unchaperoned, in his house.

It had not seemed wrong.

In fact she could not think of anything that had happened that could be misconstrued by anyone as being wrong since the Duke had taken her away from the Moulin Rouge.

The whole house, like him, seemed to be haloed with a beauty that made her think of her mother and the atmosphere there had been in their home outside Paris.

But she knew quite well what the parents of the girls with whom she had been at School would think, if any of their daughters behaved in such a manner.

Although she asked herself helplessly, what else she could have done, she knew it was something that must not continue.

Now she was not thinking of herself, but of the Duke.

As Viceroy of Ireland, he would represent the Queen and Her Majesty stood for everything that was respectable and conventional. That certainly did not include a young woman with no money and nowhere to go.

"What shall I . . . do? Tell me . . . Mama, what . . . shall I do?" Una asked.

But for once her prayer was not a desperate plea for help, simply because the Duke's kiss had made her pulsate as if to hidden music, and she felt that the whole world shone with a celestial light.

She undressed slowly and got into bed.

As she did so, she asked herself why she could not have stayed with him for just a little while longer, then perhaps he would have kissed her again.

'Tomorrow he will leave me to go back to London,' she decided.

She hid her face in the pillow because it was an agony to think of parting from him.

"I love him! I love him!" she cried over and over again.

She thought she would lie awake and listen for him to come up the stairs and go to his bedroom next door to hers.

She was aware that there was a communicating door between them, but it had meant nothing to her, except that he was near, and because of it she felt safe.

She knew that even to hear his footsteps would make her feel as if his arms were around her again and she need no longer be afraid.

She left one candle burning by her bed so that she would not fall asleep, then went back in her mind over everything that had happened during the evening.

Their dinner at the *Grand Vefour*, the things they had said to each other, the drive in the open carriage, the lights in the Place de la Concorde, the shimmering silver of the Seine.

It had all been an enchantment that was like a fairy-story but she knew this one would not have a happy ending.

Yet it had been a happiness beyond words, beyond the wildest heights of her imagination, to feel his lips on hers, the strength of his arms and the closeness of him.

"I will pray for him all my life," she vowed, "pray that he will help other people as he has . . . helped me, and that the Irish will benefit by his brilliant mind and his generous heart."

Thinking of the Duke, she must have drifted away into a dream in which her head was on his shoulder, as it had been when they drove close together in the carriage.

She was suddenly conscious that she was no longer dreaming, but was awake and the door of her bedroom had opened.

She heard it hazily, not wishing to lose her dream and the feeling that she was close to the Duke.

Then she heard a thick voice ask:

"Are you — a — shleep, pretty lady?"

Una started and opened her eyes.

Standing inside the open door was Lord Stanton, and even before she looked at him, she knew by the way he slurred his words, that he was drunk.

She had seen her father drunk on several occasions in the past, which had shocked and frightened her. But it was very much more frightening to find Lord Stanton in her room and see the smile on his lips.

"Came — say goo'-night," he said, "an' kiss one of the prettiesht little sladies — ever se' eyes on!"

Una sat up in bed.

"Go away!" she said. "You have . . . no right to . . . come into my . . . room!"

She meant to sound firm and angry, but instead, her voice trembled and she could speak hardly above a whisper.

"Looked all over Parish," Lord Stanton said, swaying as he spoke, "an' never foun' anyone's pretty ash — you!"

He spluttered over the last words, then added:

"You c'n make up for my dish-appointment — an' kish me goo'-night."

"No . . . no . . . !" Una exclaimed.

He was lurching towards her, his hands outstretched.

"No . . . no . . . !" she cried again.

She realised he was not listening and was almost at her side. Then she remembered that on the other side of the room was the door that would lead her to the Duke.

At that moment it was like a lifebuoy to a drowning man, and with a little stifled scream as she felt the touch of Lord Stanton's hot hands, she scrambled across the bed onto the floor on the other side.

Then without looking back, she rushed towards the communicating door and pulled it open.

It was heavy, far heavier than she had anticipated, but she used all her strength to open it and as she managed it, she heard Lord Stanton call out even as she was free of him.

Because she was so frightened, she rushed through the door.

Only when she did so, did she find that she was not in the Duke's bedroom as she had expected to be, but in a very small space, which in a previous age, might have been used as a powder-closet.

There was an un-curtained window and in the dim light coming through it, she saw another door straight ahead.

She hurled herself against it. It opened inwards and she fell, rather than walked into the room beyond.

The Duke turned round in astonishment as the door opened and Una, breathless with fear, flung herself against him.

For the moment she could not speak, she could hardly breathe and as his arms went round her, she clung to him convulsively.

"What has happened? What has upset you?" the Duke asked.

He could feel her trembling through the thin lawn of her nightgown and he thought, as his arms tightened, that it was fate that she should have come to him, when he had been so determined not to go to her.

"What has happened?" he asked again and now, still breathless, her voice coming jerkily from between her lips, Una answered:

"Th-that . . . man . . . your cousin . . . he . . . he frightened me!"

"Frightened you? How could he do that?" the Duke asked sharply.

"He said he wanted . . . to . . . k-kiss me," Una whispered.

She hid her face against the Duke again, knowing because she was with him, that she was safe and Lord Stanton could not touch her.

"This is something I will not have happen in my house!" the Duke exclaimed angrily.

He made a movement as if he would go towards the door Una had left open, but she clung to him crying:

"No, no! Do not . . . leave me! And there must not . . . be a row!"

"Why not?" the Duke asked harshly. "It is intolerable that any man should behave in such a manner."

Even as he spoke he knew that it was his own fault.

He had made it clear to Bertie Stanton that Una was nothing of importance in his life, and as she was staying alone in the house, what was he likely to think, except that she was a loose woman, without any moral principles?

Una was right. It would be a mistake to make a scene.

He merely held her close against him, knowing that she had decided the question which had confronted him for the last two hours.

263

He loved her, and he could not, whatever the consequences, leave her alone and unprotected.

"You are safe, my darling," he said gently. "No-one shall insult you like that again."

He felt a little of her tension leave her, but she was still trembling as she raised her face to his.

By the soft light that stood beside her bed, she looked so lovely that, for a moment, he could only look at her before very gently his lips found hers.

He kissed her and as he did so, he realised she was no longer trembling, but quivering once again, with the ecstasy he had evoked in her before.

His mouth held her captive until he felt as if they were both floating above the world in an enchantment which he had never known before.

When he raised his head, he looked down at her again and said, his voice unsteady:

"I love you, my precious one, and I intend to look after you, and you will never be afraid again."

There was an expression of radiance on her face before she said, a little hesitatingly:

"I do not . . . understand . . . you said it was . . . impossible for me to be . . . with you."

"I am asking you to marry me," the Duke said very quietly. "And nothing in the world is more important than that you should be my wife."

Una gave a little cry of sheer happiness.

Then he was kissing her again, kissing her wildly, fiercely, passionately until the softness of her lips responded to his and he knew she loved him as overwhelmingly as he loved her.

Only when she could speak in breathless, disjointed little words did Una say:

"I love . . . you! I love you . . . and I never thought . . . I would be able to . . . tell you so."

"I love you!" the Duke said, "and I have every intention of telling you so a million times, for the rest of our lives."

"Is it . . . true? Can you . . . really . . . love me . . . ?"

"I have never known love until this moment," the Duke said. "Now I have found it, as I have found you and know it is irresistible."

Una drew a deep breath, then she said hesitatingly:

"Perhaps it is . . . wrong for you to . . . love me . . . wrong for you . . . I mean."

The Duke did not speak and she went on:

"You should marry somebody . . . grand

". . . especially as you are to be a . . . Viceroy."

"I am not going to be a Viceroy," the Duke replied. "I am going to marry you, and we are going to be so happy together that nothing else in the world is of any importance."

He felt Una stiffen.

"Are you . . . telling me," she asked, "that because you . . . marry me . . . you will not be able to be . . . Viceroy?"

The fear was back in her voice and because the Duke did not wish her to be alarmed, he said quickly:

"I have no wish to be a Viceroy. I want to lead an ordinary, quiet life, and I want no other position, except that of being your husband."

Una looked up at his face, then she put both her hands on his chest to push him a little way from her.

"It is . . . not right," she said. "I know it is not right for you. You are so . . . clever . . . so brilliant . . . and I was thinking tonight when I went to bed, how much you will be able to . . . help the Irish."

"Forget the Irish!" the Duke said sharply. "They are of no importance. It is you who matters and I love you. It will take a very long time, my precious, to tell you how much."

He would have kissed her again, but her hands still held him away from her.

"No," she said. "No! I cannot . . . allow you to do . . . this. I love you . . . too much."

She made an unexpected movement and freed herself from the Duke's arms to move away from him and sit down on the side of the big bed.

The Duke made no effort to prevent her leaving him. He only watched her with a tender expression in his eyes, that no-one had ever seen before.

He knew that in the whole of his life he had never known a woman who had put his interests in front of her own.

He knew too there was not one woman of his acquaintance who would not be wildly ambitious, not only to be the Duchess of Wolstanton, but also the Vicereine of Ireland.

As Una sat there thinking, she had no idea what a beautiful picture she made.

In her plain white nightgown she was silhouetted against the crimson silk curtains which draped the Duke's bed and which had been chosen by his grandfather when he decorated the house.

There was the huge coat-of-arms of the Wolstanton family embroidered in brilliant colours on the bedback, and the Duke thought that she looked like some nymph who had stepped out of a fairy-tale and was too ethereal to be human.

"I . . . have to . . . think," she said, almost as if she spoke to herself.

"That is where you are mistaken," the Duke replied. "Let your husband, as I intend to be, do all the thinking from now on. All you have to do, my beautiful one, is to love me."

He moved slowly towards her, then as she turned her little worried face up to his, he said:

"You have been through enough for today. Go to sleep and tomorrow I will solve all our problems quite simply, because we will be married, and you will be my wife."

She shook her head and he said with a smile on his lips:

"I shall make my wife obey me."

As he spoke he put out his arms and lifted her up from the bed to hold her tightly against him.

"I am . . . trying to think what is . . . right for you," Una murmured.

He held her closer still and answered:

"It is right for you to kiss me."

She was about to speak but he closed her lips with his.

Then as he knew that she was as thrilled

as he was, it was difficult to think of anything but each other.

Only when they had once again left the
world behind and felt a rapture that was
beyond thought, did the Duke come back to
earth and say:

"My darling, you must go to sleep. I will
take you back to your room."

As if she only now remembered the
reason why she had run to him, he felt a
little shiver go through her and he said
quickly:

"There will be no-one there to frighten
you and we will leave the doors open so that
I can hear if you call."

He smiled so that there was no rebuke in
his words as he said:

"You should have remembered to lock
your door."

"I . . . never thought of it," Una said
simply, "we were not allowed to lock our
doors at the Convent."

The Duke wondered as she spoke how he
could ever have doubted her innocence and
her purity.

It had never even struck her, he knew,
that she should be self-conscious and shy
because she had run to him just as she was
in her nightgown.

He thought, as he touched her hair with

his lips, that he was the most fortunate man in the world, because he had found what all men seek in a woman, but so few find.

"I will take you back," he said quietly.

He bent down and picked Una up in his arms.

"You have enough to worry about for to-night," he said. "I am going to carry you to bed, my precious, and I want you to go to sleep thinking only of me."

"It would be . . . impossible to do . . . anything else," she answered.

"Tomorrow night we will be together," he said softly, "and I will tell you of my love and you shall tell me of yours."

He carried her as he spoke, through the powder-closet and into her own bedroom. He felt the softness of her body and the fragrance of her hair gave him sensations he had never known.

In the light still burning by the bed Una could see that the room was empty and the door into the passage closed.

The Duke laid her down against the pillows and pulled the bed-clothes over her. Then he sat down facing her to say:

"I love you! And I want you to know, my lovely darling, that although we cannot go to Ireland, I am happy to live with you in England, France or anywhere else in the world you choose."

Una reached up her arms and put them round his neck.

"You are . . . so wonderful . . . so clever," she said. "It is really a . . . waste of you, for me to have . . . you all to myself. But . . . please promise me . . . one thing?"

"What is that?" the Duke asked.

"That you will let me try to . . . help you just a . . . little in . . . everything you do. I will not be a nuisance . . . I will not impose myself on you . . . but I do want to be a part . . . a real part of your life."

The Duke held her very close.

"You will always be that," he said, "the part of my life that really matters, the part which is also a part of me, because, my precious little love, we will not be two people, but one."

His lips found hers as he spoke and because he had been deeply moved by what she said, Una knew that his kiss was somehow sacred.

The Duke swept her away into the light that seemed to envelop them both with a glory that was almost blinding.

This was love, a love which pulsated through her body and her mind. A love she had thought she must lose.

Her arms pulled him a little closer and she

knew as their kiss joined them in an ecstasy that came from God, that never again would she be frightened, lonely, or alone in Paris or anywhere else.

The Duke awoke and was aware that he was happier than he ever remembered being in his life before.

He knew everything had changed simply because Una had come into his life. She was what he had always imagined was unattainable, and yet had remained an ideal that was too perfect to be translated into ordinary living.

All the women he had known and with whom he had spent so much of his time seemed, in retrospect, a waste of himself and his brains. But he knew it was more than that.

It had been a betrayal of his own standards and of his own needs.

Una fulfilled in him something which was so intrinsically a part of himself that he wondered now how he could have existed without her.

He rose from his bed and walked across the room to stand at the open door which communicated with hers.

He resisted an impulse to go to her and kiss her awake.

He told himself that she needed sleep after all the traumatic experiences of yesterday, and he must think of her rather than himself.

He closed the door very quietly, then rang for his valet.

The sunshine was glinting on the trees in the garden and he thought, as he looked from the window that it was just the sort of wedding-day he would wish to have and which would envelop Una with a golden haze.

He was nearly dressed when there was a knock on the door and when his valet opened it Mr Beaumont came into the room.

The Duke who was brushing his hair with two ivory-backed brushes turned to look at him in surprise.

"You are early, Beaumont!" he remarked, "but actually I was just going to send for you."

"Dubucheron is here," Mr Beaumont replied. "And he brought you this."

He walked across the room as he spoke and held out a copy of *Le Jour*.

A paragraph low down on the page had been heavily outlined.

The Duke took it and said:

"I suppose Dubucheron is looking for money. Give him a thousand pounds. He has earned it!"

"A thousand pounds?" Mr Beaumont exclaimed. "Surely that is too much!"

The Duke did not reply and his Comptroller realised he did not intend to have an argument on the matter. He was also reading the marked newspaper.

The item was headed:

"A LOST HEIR"

"Mr. Caulder and Mr. Stephens, Senior partners of the well-known London firm of Solicitors, Messrs. Caulder, Stephens and Culthorpe, arrived in Paris yesterday to visit Montmartre. They are not, however, interested in seeing the pictures of our younger artists which have attracted the attention of the artistic world. Instead they are looking for one artist in particular, who, they think, may have a Studio in Montmartre.

It was announced last month that Lord Dorset had died unexpectedly at the age of fifty-three. He was unmarried and the Solicitors to the estate are now searching for his younger brother, Mr. Julius Thornton who will inherit not only the title, but a large estate.

Lord Dorset's brother left England nineteen years ago when he resigned from his

Regiment, the Grenadier Guards, and at the same time, eloped with the daughter of Sir Robert Marlow. This caused a great deal of excitement at the time and his father, the previous Lord Dorset, cut off all communication with his son, as did Sir Robert Marlow with his daughter.

It is believed, however, that Mr. Julius Thornton took up painting, for which he had already shown a considerable talent, and settled in France.

He may have changed his name, but the Solicitors are confident that if, as is considered a possibility, he is still living in France, he will undoubtedly be known amongst his contemporaries in Montmartre."

The Duke read the paragraph to the end, then handing the newspaper back to Mr Beaumont, he said:

"Tell Dubucheron to bring the gentlemen concerned to see me tomorrow morning."

"Tomorrow?" Mr Beaumont questioned.

"I shall be too busy to see them today," the Duke said, "and so will you."

His Comptroller waited, a slightly puzzled expression in his eyes.

"First," the Duke said, picking up his hair-brushes, "I want you to go to the Rue de la Paix and tell two or more of the best Couturiers to bring here immediately, the prettiest very small sized gowns they have ready, together with hats to match."

Mr Beaumont's eyes widened but he did not speak, and the Duke continued:

"Having done that, will you go to La Mairie and arrange for my marriage to take place at twelve noon?"

"Your marriage?" Mr Beaumont ejaculated.

Now the expression of astonishment on his face was almost ludicrous.

"I understand a Civil Marriage is compulsory in France," the Duke said, "but we will follow it with a short Service at the British Embassy Church."

With difficulty Mr Beaumont found his voice.

"I must congratulate Your Grace," he said. "This is certainly a surprise!"

The Duke smiled at him mischievously.

It always pleased him to surprise his Comptroller and this time he had certainly succeeded.

He put down his hair-brushes and turned round.

"Hurry, Beaumont."

"I shall need to do that," his Comptroller said, "and having reached the cross-roads you have certainly made a decision."

"Have you decided whether it is right or left?" the Duke asked.

"I may be wrong," Mr Beaumont smiled, "but I think you have followed the dictates of your heart, and that could not be anything but right."

The Duke laughed, and it was a sound of almost boyish exuberance.

"That is exactly what I have done!"

Mr Beaumont walked towards the door.

"I will give your message to Dubucheron, Your Grace, then leave immediately for the Rue de la Paix."

"I shall need you as a witness at my wedding," the Duke said, "and no-one else."

"I am honoured," Mr Beaumont murmured.

He had the door open when the Duke stopped him.

"Beaumont."

"Yes, Your Grace?"

The Duke picked up a letter which was lying on top of the dressing-table.

"If you have any time left today," he said, "you can draft out an answer to the Prime Minister."

He threw the letter and it spun in the air to fall at Mr Beaumont's feet, and as he bent to pick it up, the Duke said:

"Tell him I will be very honoured for him to put forward my name to Her Majesty, for the appointment of Viceroy of Ireland, and that I and my wife will do our best for that long-suffering country."

There was a smile of gratification on Mr Beaumont's face as he went from the room carrying the Prime Minister's letter in his hand, but the Duke did not see it.

He had walked to the window to look out once again at the sunlit garden.

He knew that what he had read in *Le Jour* would make everything much simpler and much easier in the future, not so much for him as for Una.

It was her happiness of which he was thinking and he was concerned that her Dorset relations would be only too glad to welcome her as the Duchess of Wolstanton, as would her mother's family.

It was an incredible piece of good luck that this should have happened at this particular moment.

But as far as the Duke was concerned he could only think of one thing, and that was Una.

He loved her and he was relieved at what he had learnt of her family, not from his own point of view, but from hers.

He would have been quite happy, in fact

very happy, to spend his life quite quietly, just looking after her, protecting her and preventing her from feeling lonely.

But he knew they both had the intelligent capacity to ask for more in their lives than just themselves.

The challenge that awaited them in Ireland was something that they could face together and it would fulfil and develop them both.

He remembered how last night, she had asked him to promise that he would let her help him a little in everything he did.

He knew now it would not be a little he would ask of her, but a lot. For he was aware that, young though she was, she had a depth of character that was unusual and would not only help him, but guide and inspire him for the rest of their life together.

As he looked out into the garden, the sun seemed almost dazzling in its brilliance and the Duke hoped that was how their life would be: brilliant not only for themselves but for the people they could help.

It was Una who had effected already a change and a difference in his life, giving it a sense of purpose and a potential that had not been there before.

He felt himself longing for her with an intensity that made him feel that he was calling her name aloud.

"I love you! God, how much I love you, my precious!" he said, as if she was standing beside him.

Then for the first time for many years, the Duke added a prayer.

"Thank you, God, for letting me find her."